# HATING MR. WRITE

## A MR. SERIES NOVELLA

BREANNA LYNN

ISBN: 978-1-955359-52-8 (eBook)

ISBN: 978-1-955359-53-5 (paperback)

Cover By: Kate Farlow with Y'all. That Graphic.

Edited by: Happily Editing Anns and VB Proofreads

Printed in United States of America

https://breannalynnauthor.com

## MR. RIGHT ISN'T ALWAYS FICTIONAL...

As a single mom of two, my me-time is sacred—filled with late nights lost in every romance novel I can find. When I volunteer to help my best friend plan her small-town wedding, I'm bracing for quiet days and cozy nights. Real-life romance? Definitely not on my agenda.

Then there's Jagger Brooks—my grumpy, cocky summer neighbor who's equal parts maddening and magnetic. He's nothing like the heroes in my books… or so I thought.

But beneath that playboy exterior, Jagger hides a sweet, unexpected heart. And when sparks ignite between us, I'm caught up in a passion I never saw coming—one that feels straight out of my favorite stories.

I'm only here for the summer. Falling isn't an option—not for a man I barely know.

Can I trust Jagger with my heart, or is this summer fling destined to be just another chapter I close too soon?

*To Isabelle—*
*Thank you for requiring the perfect day...*

# CHAPTER 1

## JAGGER

*In short, I wanted to like JA Hart's latest release. I tried. So many of my friends told me how much they loved the first two books he released last year. Not to mention his other series that I added to my TBR, knowing I'd read them only if I enjoyed this one. But the heroine in* The Reality of Love *was anything but real. From her whiny conversations to the way the hero always had to rescue her, she came across as little more than a victim of her situation—and I can't forget the superfluous number of sex scenes that left me questioning JA's experiences with real-life women. Obviously he has no idea how to please a woman—be they reader or lover.        . I cannot in good conscience recommend this book. Hopefully, I'll have better news about this next read. Until next time! XOXO, Rocky Mountain Romance Reader*

"What crawled up her ass and died?"

This is what I get for reading my reviews. If I could, I'd crumple up the review and toss the wadded-up paper in the trash. The physical release would do me some good. Clicking on the little X in the top left corner of the internet browser window doesn't give me the same satisfaction, but it'll have to do.

With a huff, I kick out of my desk chair and pace the small bedroom I use as my office. Maybe the movement will calm the wheels in my head and keep them from spinning off track into a spiral of imposter syndrome.

"You never should have looked at the reviews." My voice echoes against the walls.

I know better. It was one of the first pieces of advice I was given when I started indie publishing. But I have a thick skin—owning the town's only bar means I deal with a lot of drunk assholes—so reading my reviews has never been a problem before. The majority are good with occasional one- or two-star reviews from readers who like to go on about why it's wrong for a man to write romance.

But this blogger has made it her life's mission to single-handedly destroy my day. She's got twenty-five thousand followers and she's left glowing reviews for every other book she's read this year. But mine? She can't *in good conscience* recommend it? Her words ricochet through me, making it impossible to get my head on straight and write this next book.

*Oh, yeah, because you were writing so much before you scrolled social media?*

I don't even have to look at my computer screen for my work-in-progress's word count.

Zero isn't a hard number to remember.

Blowing out a breath, I tip my head back and stare at the ceiling.

"Think, jackass. This should be a cakewalk at this point." I haven't typed a single word, and still, this book has been more of a challenge than writing the previous six combined.

I snap up straight when my phone vibrates against my desk and cross the small room to pick it up.

SHEP

Did Jade's friend show up next door?

2

Fuck, I was so focused on this book and the review bomb that I'd forgotten. Jade's friend is coming from Colorado Springs and renting the Airbnb next door. During the last ski season, it became a revolving door of single women in for a weekend of winter fun. If that fun included a night of no-strings sex? I wasn't complaining.

Something told me I wouldn't have the same relationship with this temporary neighbor.

Nope.

Did you check?

Dammit. Stepping closer to the window, I check the driveway, snap a picture, and text it to Shep.

See? Not here yet.

Cranky much?

Am I keeping you from your beauty sleep?

Not quite. Despite closing at the bar last night, I've been up for hours. The five hours of sleep I managed plus the three cups of coffee I've pounded mean I'm more than awake. I'm so alert I'm practically hovering off the ground. But staring at the blinking cursor of death for an hour before falling down the review hole has taken its toll. *Rocky Mountain Romance Reader* wasn't the only one who had some...let's say *strong* opinions about *The Reality of Love*. She was just the most vocal.

Who says I was sleeping?

Maybe I was entertaining? ::wink emoji::

You could give lessons on how to be a man-whore.

3

> Seriously, though, please limit the "entertaining" when Jade's friend is there.
>
> I'd rather not stress my fiancée out any more than she already is.

> > ::middle finger emoji::
> >
> > Why is it that your marriage means I'm getting cock-blocked?

> Jagger...
>
> Just for me? Okay? I'm asking as your best friend.

He had to play that card. Fuck. He's been my best friend for almost fifteen years. And despite what he thinks, my disinterest in settling down doesn't make me a man-whore. I'm happy he finally pulled his head out of his ass when it comes to Jade, but that doesn't mean I'm ready to dive into a life of committed monogamy alongside him. He'd still be mooning over her from afar if it hadn't been for me. But it doesn't mean I can't fuck with him.

> > Fine. It's only a week, right?

> 3 weeks.

> > She's here the whole time???

> I told you that already.

Huh. Nope. I have no recollection of that tidbit of information.

When no response comes, I key in another message.

> > Be glad you're my best friend. I wouldn't do this for anybody else.

Yes, I know.

I appreciate it.

It's also why you're my best man.

                                    Any cute bridesmaids?

Son of a bitch.

                                    Can't blame a guy for trying.

If it's you? Yes, I can.

Keep it in your pants.

Or at least away from the wedding party.

                                    Spoilsport.


I'm grinning for the first time all morning. I love yanking his chain.

And one more thing.

                                    Fuck. Now what?

Jade's friend is off-limits.

                                    Not going to be a problem.

I have no desire to get involved with a woman who will be staying next door for three entire weeks. Even innocent flirting can become fodder for a stage-five clinger, and I have no interest in dealing with that headache.

I have game. But drama is not the name of that game.

My phone vibrates twice in quick succession.

The first text is from Shep.

It better not be.

Rolling my eyes, I click on the second new message. It's from Becky, the woman who handles the lunch shift at Expedition Brewing.

BECKY

You busy?

With a sigh, I shake my head and close my useless laptop.

No. What's up?

Before she can respond, I'm heading to the shower. I have a feeling I know where that question is leading.

The babysitter just called. Levi is running a fever and I need to go pick him up.

I crank the knob and let the water heat while I respond.

Anybody in for lunch yet?

Becky covers the lunch crowd, which gives me a break so I'm not working eighty hours a week like I did when I first bought the bar.

Though it looks like I'll be there a little more than normal for the next few days.

No.

Have Phil keep an eye up front.

Phil may be an excellent cook, but his specialty is not customer service.

I'll be there in 30.

The book is going to have to wait.

*Writer's Block—1, Jagger—0.*

Writer's block has more on me than that, but I refuse to acknowledge it.

Time to go do something I can actually succeed at today.

# CHAPTER 2

## HAYLEY

"*Hey*, Mom?"

It takes all my energy not to cringe at my sweet, and very curious, five-year-old's voice. In my defense, even the most patient person can only take so many *Hey, Mom*s before teetering on the edge of sanity. My patience frayed at the two-hour mark of our almost six-hour trip from Colorado Springs to Aspen Falls, Colorado.

But it's not Maisie's fault that the GPS didn't account for traffic snarls and the myriad of construction zones along the route. And Teddy can't help but bounce from one side of my Subaru to the other. The way he fixes his big brown eyes on me when he begs for a bathroom break and leg stretch would be adorable if any of my patience was still intact. The one-year-old goldendoodle is still a puppy. One with energy I hadn't considered when we started this endeavor.

The only one who hasn't made himself known is Declan.

I glance in the rearview mirror to check on my sullen twelve-year-old, wishing for some sign of consciousness besides the steady flick of his thumb on the screen and the head bop to whatever is blasting in his headphones.

"Mom."

Shit.

"Yeah, baby doll?" I try to smile, but I'm sure it comes across as a grimace.

Thank God I'm facing the road so they can't see my face.

"Why are some of the trees pointy and some aren't?"

The question catches me so completely off guard that I nearly choke on the cold coffee I'm guzzling. Cold or not, the blessed cup holds the nectar of the gods keeping me going after what should have been a three-hour drive.

"Huh?"

Her responding exhale is deep and speaks of long-suffering indignity the way only a five-year-old can sound.

"The trees. Some of them have pointy sticks. And the others have leaves."

"We have both kinds of trees at home too. Remember what I told you about those?" I ask.

Her face brightens in the rearview mirror. "Oh yeah!" She squeezes Teddy's neck, and the puppy squirms against the affection.

"Mais." I keep my voice calm despite the irritation that's climbing through me with every passing mile.

"Huh?"

Teddy's squirms are growing more frantic, but Maisie ignores him.

"Baby, make sure Teddy can breathe."

"Oops, sorry, Teddy Bear." A sheepish grin covers her face. She releases the dog, who instantly licks her face in forgiveness.

Her expression right now—the unfiltered joy mixed with the sweet little girl—makes all the years I spent with my ex worth it. And it gives me the fortitude necessary to deal with the sullen pre-teen in the seat next to her.

I assess Declan again. He's slumped as low in his seat as his seatbelt will allow, his attention focused on the device in his hand.

"Declan." I raise my voice to be heard over the music playing through his headphones.

And try not to think about the damage he's surely doing to his hearing.

He doesn't glance up, thumb still flicking at the screen.

I try again.

"Declan."

Eyes that are a carbon copy of his dad's meet mine in the mirror.

*Rob, why can't you spend more time with your son?*

Declan tugs one side of his headphones back.

"What?"

"Are you doing okay? Do you need to go potty?"

"I'm not five." His words are a snarl.

My stomach sinks. What happened to my sweet little boy who was just as inquisitive as Maisie once upon a time?

I pull in a deep breath through my nose and release it slowly, lifting a hand to the back of my neck to rub at the tension that's been building for hours.

"Bud, I'm just checking to see if you need me to stop before we get to the house."

My best friend, Jade, set us up with an adorable rental for the three weeks before her wedding. And she talked the owners into renting it for half its usual rate since she'd taught both their kids when they were in high school.

"How long until we get there?"

That sentence is the longest he's spoken to me all day. Every other interaction has been limited to looks, grunts, and mono-syllables.

I shift my attention to the GPS.

"According to this"—I tap on its screen— "twenty minutes."

"I can wait." With that, he shifts the headphones back into place and drops his attention back to his phone.

Okay, then.

My heart breaks for the little boy who still exists inside that gangly tween body. He hasn't told me as much, but he misses his dad. The two of them weren't super close—it's hard for a man to be close to his children when he works eighty-hour weeks and spends his off time having an affair—but that doesn't make the lack of interaction with his dad any easier. Declan doesn't know about any of the bad shit. The last thing I want to do is sway his opinion of the man.

I hoped that Rob was serious when he said he wanted to see the kids two weekends a month. But in the six months since our divorce was finalized, he's only seen them once. Shortly after the ink had dried on our divorce decree, he took them to the park for an hour. He called Declan on his birthday two months ago, and we haven't heard from him since. Not even on Maisie's birthday last month.

Music plays quietly through the speakers. The only station I could find was a country station. Even though I don't normally listen to this kind of music, I've liked several of the songs that have played. It beats silence. Or the level of silence I get while Maisie chatters to Teddy explaining how some of the trees outside look like our Christmas tree at home.

A green sign on the side of the road catches my attention.

*Aspen Falls. Elevation 9,423 feet. Population 7,851.*

The light at the end of the tunnel of this problematic car ride is in sight and relief floods my body. I still have to go buy groceries for the next few weeks, but first we'll get to the house and unpack. As if sensing he'll soon be released from the prison of this moving vehicle, Teddy whines and bounces between the two windows in the back.

"Mom!"

"Teddy!"

Both kids yell simultaneously, and in response, my fingers tighten around the steering wheel.

"We're almost there." I grit out the words as a mantra more to myself than to calm the kids or the puppy down.

Following the directions of the GPS, I turn at the outskirts of the town and ease down the winding dirt road until it opens to a clearing on the side of a small lake. Two houses sit side by side before it. Which one was it? 4142 or 4124?

I pull into the driveway of the first one and turn to Declan.

"Please take Teddy and your sister for a w-a-l-k."

I don't dare say the word or Teddy will go more ballistic than he already is.

Declan rolls his eyes, but clips Teddy's leash to his collar without argument. On the other side of the car, Maisie unbuckles, then they exit in a flurry of happy barks, giggles, and gangly limbs.

They wander toward the back of the second house and stop when Teddy sniffs around the base of a tree.

"They'll be fine," I tell myself.

The quiet of the car settles over me and eases some of the strain in my shoulders. I give myself the span of several breaths before I snag the slip of paper with the code for the door out of the second cup holder and head for the house.

"1704," I mutter as I type the numbers into the keypad.

A red light flashes, and when I turn the knob, the door doesn't open.

I double-check the Post-it note. Sure enough, I had the numbers right—I asked if I could use the kids' birthday as the code.

*1704.*

"Okay, Hayley, let's try this again."

Slower this time, more deliberate, I press the corresponding keys.

Still nothing.

"Shit."

I jiggle the handle with a little more force than the first time.

Nothing. And the blinds are closed, so I can't peer in.

"One more time. Third time's the charm and all that."

Squaring my shoulders, I poke at all four numbers and shake the handle as I push into the door.

I'm still leaning against it when it's yanked open, and I trip into the doorway. I manage to twist on the way down and land on my ass rather than my hip, but the jolt takes my breath away. All I register from where I sit on the floor is a pair of hairy legs and bare feet in front of me.

"What the fuck?"

The deep voice barely registers before I'm unceremoniously hefted back into a standing position.

"You alright there, gorgeous? Women fall at my feet all the time, sure, but not literally," he says with a smirk.

It's the smirk that makes my blood boil. The facial expression is so similar to Rob's that my palms itch with the need to slap it off his face.

*He's not Rob.*

But based on his quick line and the devil-may-care smile that resembles that of Ian Somerhalder's character on one of my favorite TV shows, he *is* a playboy.

And he's standing in front of me in nothing but a low-slung navy towel. His hair is slicked back, and he smells like a mix of spiced bergamot, sandalwood, and a seductive cologne meant to drop panties wherever he travels.

Mine are staying firmly in place, thank you.

"Why are you in our house?" I ask. The words come out direct, but calm.

"Last time I checked, my name was on the mortgage, sweetheart."

He crosses sculpted arms—the epitome of arm porn, if I'm being honest—across an equally impressive tattooed chest and leans back against the jamb like he has all the time in the world. The lines on his abdomen deepen and the towel looks ready to give way.

I hate the not-so-small part of me that wishes it would. And I scold the way my body heats, and not in anger, at the sight. Garnering my self-control, I transform that reaction into annoyance.

"My name isn't 'gorgeous' or 'sweetheart,'" I tell him with a glare.

He lifts his hands in apology but the smirk stays firmly in place.

"My apologies, Queen..." He tilts his head like he's waiting for me to tell him my name. Not happening.

"Look, I don't know what game you're playing, buster, but my friend rented this house and we're staying here for a few weeks."

His eyes widen and the smirk slips off his face. "You're Jade's friend?"

"You know Jade?" I fire back.

He throws his head back with a laugh.

I try to ignore the flutter of attraction in my belly at the way the tendons and muscles of his neck move. He's not a gym bro, but he is toned in all the right places.

What the hell is wrong with me?

He isn't attractive. He's too much like Rob for my comfort and I have the divorce decree at home to prove that men like him are no good.

"Swee—I've known Jade since we were in first grade."

"It doesn't mean you're staying with us," I sputter, lifting my chin.

Slowly, and with one brow raised, he steps closer and points over my shoulder to the other house. The masculine heat that threads along my body is enough to tempt a nun. I turn my head and take in the two-story gray house with white shutters he's pointing at.

4142.

"You rented that one."

My anger deflates to embarrassment, and my cheeks heat.

Shoulders slumping, I swallow back my mortification. "Oh."

"You're not the first woman to wander over here accidentally," he murmurs in my ear.

I jerk my head away from him so fast I practically fall off the porch. "I'll bet. But you won't have to worry about me making that mistake again."

With that, I spin on my heel and stomp toward my car.

His responding laughter echoes across the lake. "See you around, neighbor."

I wrench open my car door and throw myself behind the wheel. With a huff, I turn the key that's still in the ignition and slam the car door.

"Like hell you will."

With a quick three-point turn, I pull into the driveway of what's going to be our home for the next few weeks. Luckily, Mr. Smirky Studmuffin is nowhere to be seen when I make it up to the front porch and key the code in successfully.

If it takes everything I have, I'll ignore my jackass neighbor for the next three weeks.

How hard can it be?

# CHAPTER 3

## JAGGER

*S*cents of vanilla and cinnamon tease my nose sweetly while warm brown eyes snap fire in my direction. Though this fire is not the kind caused by irritation. Dream neighbor has a different kind of heat leveled on me, and it's having a predictable effect on my dick. The twitch draws her attention down and her tongue peeks out to slick along her berry-colored lips.

Fuuuuuck.

She drifts closer and I glide my fingers up the smooth skin of her arms, then thread my fingers through soft brown curls that tangle around her face. A low hum vibrates from her throat as her eyes drift shut. She angles closer and tips her head back, offering her lips to me.

Closing my eyes, I pull her in. Her breasts crush against my chest, making my dick twitch again, as I lower my head, ready to claim her mouth. To see if she tastes as good as she smells.

Snickerdoodles and sin.

Yes, fucking, please.

We're millimeters apart when a high-pitched scream pierces

my eardrums. The image in front of me—the woman in my arms —disappears between one breathe and the next.

"Goddammit."

My dick presses so painfully against my mattress I consider taking matters into my own hand, but when another scream echoes loudly through the room, I jackknife to a sitting position.

"What the actual fuck?"

I kick off the covers and scramble for the jeans and T-shirt I kicked off at 3 a.m. when I finally made it home. After heading into the bar early, I worked the rest of the night, handling crisis after crisis. Lucky me, a group of frat brothers came to town for the evening and decided that my bar was the perfect place for drunken shenanigans.

I don't bother to grab my phone as I stumble out of my room. I almost miss the first stair but right myself before I fall down the whole flight. The third scream hits me just as I open the front door—it's a thousand times louder without the walls of the house muffling it. I don't know if my wince is from the bright sunlight or the volume of the half-pint in front of me.

The dog yapping as it runs circles around the screaming little girl only adds to the thousands of needles jabbing themselves into my brain.

"What the fu—" I stop myself in the nick of time based on the little girl's widening eyes. "Fudge is going on out here? Are you being murdered?"

The noise from both her and the dog have come to a blessed stop, but now my ears are ringing in the deafening silence.

"Well?" I ask.

She shakes her head.

"Who's responsible for you?"

I try not to fidget under the two pairs of soulful brown eyes that watch me. I'm not sure which is worse. Hers or the dog's. Hers, though, dart to the side. Then she points a finger at a kid a few years older than she is. He's hunched over a phone with a pair of headphones covering his ears. No wonder he hasn't looked up. He can't hear me and I'd bet twenty bucks he didn't hear her either.

Hands clenched at my sides, I march his way. I'm close enough to touch him before he even looks up. When he does, he jumps back, nearly falling off the tree stump he's perched on.

"Jesus." He whips off the headphones and stands. "What the fu—"

I arch one brow, and he breaks off before he can finish the sentence.

"Who are you?" I keep my hands fisted but put them on my hips, annoyance flashing through me at his obliviousness. "Where are your parents?"

"Who are you?" he counters. He puffs out his chest to appear bigger than he is.

My lips twitch, but I fight the urge to smile.

Twenty years ago, I was this kid.

"Maisie, Declan! Time for breakfast!" The woman from yesterday steps onto the front porch of the cottage with her hands cupped around her mouth.

She scans the area until she finds our unlikely trio—or are we a quartet?—and her shoulders tense. It isn't until she steps off the porch and strides our way that it hits me.

These kids are with her. They'll be here the whole time.

Three weeks.

*Fuck.*

Though they could be her niece and nephew visiting for the day, right? Or a friend's kids? Maybe another of Jade's friends too.

"Mommy!" The little girl runs toward the woman and wraps her arms around her hips in a death grip.

With that one word, any sliver of hope disintegrates. No, these kids will be spending the next three weeks here. Fantastic.

"They belong to you?" I ask.

She shuffles over to the older boy. The girl still clinging to her makes it tricky, but when she's beside him, she tries to wrap an arm around him. In response to her touch, he ducks away and walks toward the dog. The flash of hurt on her face makes me want to soothe her. To tell her that it's not her, it's just hormones and teenage attitude.

What the fuck is wrong with me?

She covers the hurt instantly and squares her shoulders as she turns her attention to me.

"Yes."

"What about that thing?" I thumb toward the dog.

The little girl bristles and lets out a grunt.

"Teddy isn't a thing." She finally pulls away from her mother and rushes the dog, giving it an exuberant hug.

Teddy, the dog. That's another name I can add to the growing list.

Teddy.

Maisie.

Declan.

And mystery woman.

Mom.

"Are the three of them going to be here the whole time you are?" I ask.

Fire sparks in those brown eyes, turning them the color of dark chocolate. It's the same fire I experienced yesterday. She's ready to do battle with me. What would those brown eyes look like if she wasn't pissed? Would they be warm and molten like in my dream?

*Dude, what the fuck is actually wrong with you? She's a mom.*

The one kind of woman I don't screw around with. Looks like Jade and Shep won't have to worry about me with her now.

"Not that it's any of your business, but yes, they are." She crosses her arms over her chest in a way that makes her breasts press upward against the scoop neck of her tank.

No, no, no, no, no. Mothers do not have breasts that make my hands itch and my mouth water. So my dick and my libido need to get themselves back in check.

"Can you keep it down over here? Keep the noise inside the house at the very least?"

She narrows her eyes and purses her lips to a thin line. But she doesn't say anything.

"And that mutt belongs on a leash. Unless you want him to get eaten by a bear."

"Mommy!" the little girl cries. The way she cowers and latches on to the dog tighter makes me regret my words. No one's seen a bear up here in a while. They tend to stay farther away from town.

Tears run down her cheeks as she buries her face in the dog's fur. Declan steps in front of her and the dog and levels me with a glare. The expression is identical to the one his mother is wearing.

Fuck. I don't even know her name.

"Thanks a lot. Are you always this much of a jackass?" She fires the words at me as she moves to comfort her daughter.

Maisie releases Teddy and squeezes her mother's neck, once again burying her face. The woman stands again, little girl in tow, and tilts her head, waiting for my answer.

"Nope." I pop the *p* and loop my thumbs in the back pockets of my jeans. "Only when I'm woken up by a screaming kid and a yapping mutt."

"Not a mutt," Maisie sobs, lifting her tearstained face from her mother's shoulder.

Jade's friend—because I'm not going to keep referring to her as a mother—rubs along the back of Maisie's pink T-shirt. Her expression softens as she speaks to her.

"It's okay, baby. I know. He's not a mutt."

The little girl's sobs quiet and only then does the woman fix her attention back on me.

"Listen, Mr…" She raises her brows, signaling me to supply my name.

"Brooks. Jagger Brooks."

"Mr. Brooks. Let's agree that you'll stay over there and we'll stay over here and I'll be sure that we don't bother you again."

"Thank—"

"But if you think for one second you can act like a dickhead toward me, my children, or my dog because you feel like it, you've got another thing coming." She stands straighter and hefts her daughter higher on her hip. "So take your grumpy ass back to your place because, quite honestly, the sight of you and your wounded bear slash hungover look is making me lose my appetite."

Her words and the steel in her spine surprise me enough that I hold up my hands and retreat. I don't dare turn my back on her as I go, but she doesn't wait for me to leave. Without another word, she nods toward the house for Declan to follow and heads that way. The kid follows surprisingly well for such a surly little shit. The dog looks at me and thumps his tail once before following the three humans.

"Well, fuck me," I murmur.

Looks like Mama Bear has a take-no-shit attitude.

So why does that make her that much more attractive?

🏔 🏔 🏔

"Do you have to be an asshat all the time? Or do you do it just to fuck up my life?" Shep asks when he barges into the bar several hours later.

"Huh?" I glance up from the inventory spreadsheet I've got pulled up on my tablet.

Shep sighs and drags a hand through his hair.

"Hayley called Jade."

"I don't know who that is."

"She's your neighbor, asshole. The one renting the cottage."

Hayley. That's her name. It fits her.

*How the fuck would you know?*

I've been having this argument with myself all day. I'll find myself thinking about her even while I'm actively trying not to. I do feel bad about making the little girl—Maisie—cry. I don't usually go out of my way to scare kids. I typically ignore them. And their mothers.

It's never been an issue, so surely I can continue over the next few weeks.

"It's not like she introduced herself."

"When was she supposed to do that? When you were making Maisie cry? You and I both fucking know that there hasn't been a bear spotted close to town in years."

"I do feel bad about that," I admit, scratching at the scruff on my jaw.

"You fucking should. You should also feel bad about the whole Don Juan scene when she showed up."

"The fuck? She tried to walk into my house, and I'd just gotten out of the shower. There was nothing planned there."

And if I thought about it after she fell into the doorway? I'll keep that to myself. I don't need to give Shep another reason to be pissed off right now.

"I know you well enough to know you *always* have a plan for getting laid."

"Not in this case. Moms are a no-go for me."

"For once," he mumbles.

I fist my hands at my sides and will myself to keep my voice level. "What?"

"Nothing. Seriously though, man, you've got to cut her a break. Jade said she's had a shitty-ass couple of years. She could really use the vacation."

"What do you mean 'a shitty-ass couple of years'?"

Shep shrugs and drops onto the barstool across from me. "Jade didn't say. I know Hayley is divorced, but that's it."

"You want a beer?" I hold up a bottle of his favorite.

He nods and swipes it from me before I can pop the cap.

I'm too preoccupied to bother helping him with it, wondering what defines a rough couple of years for my beautiful, but off-limits, neighbor. My curiosity is piqued. And as an author? It never bodes well.

"I should probably apologize." I grab my own bottle from the cooler and remove the cap.

Shep lowers his bottle from his lips and lifts an eyebrow. "When have you ever apologized?"

"When I'm wrong," I tell him.

"As long as I've known you, you've never apologized."

"I've never been wrong before."

Shep barks out a laugh and takes another drink. "Yeah, right. You've been wrong plenty. And the words 'I'm sorry' have never crossed your lips."

"Maybe I want to smooth things over with Jade's friend."

"Jagger." His tone is full of warning.

I hold up my free hand and shake my head. "I'm not going to do anything. I already told you. Moms and I don't mix. Think of this as my wedding present to you and Jade."

Shep rolls his eyes.

I take another pull from my beer and assess my friend. "You know what? We should do a cookout. At your house."

"My house?"

"Yeah." I dip my chin. "Invite Hayley and the kids."

"Why?" He narrows his eyes. I don't blame him. He has a right to be suspicious.

But I was telling the truth when I said moms are off-limits for me. "Why not?"

Shep only gets more wary, scanning the bar behind me, as if he'll find clues as to my motivation. "You're up to something."

"It'll be a good way to bury the hatchet between Hayley and me."

"You'll be lucky if Jade doesn't bury one between your eyes if you try anything funny."

I draw an X over the left side of my chest.

"I promise I'm not up to anything funny. I really do feel bad for making the kid cry."

"Maisie," he huffs. "Her name is Maisie."

"I feel bad for making *Maisie* cry. And the older one is no picnic either."

"Declan."

"I know their names. And the dog's. Teddy."

"Well look at you go," he says, sarcasm dripping from every word.

"Are you going to set up the cookout or not?"

With a sigh, he stands. Then he tips his bottle back and drains the rest of his beer.

"I'll talk to Jade. When do you want to do this?"

"Whenever works for you two." I swipe his empty bottle from the bar top and drop it into the recycle bin under the bar, then head back toward him. "Heading out?"

"Yeah." He fishes his keys out of his pocket. "I'm taking Jade into Boulder for dinner tonight. Some Italian place she wanted to try."

I'm glad my best friend got another chance with the love of his life. They're meant for each other. That's been clear since high school. Even if his stubbornness caused them to lose twelve years, they ultimately managed to figure it out.

"Have fun," I tell him.

He points a finger at me. "No funny business."

"Who, me?" I can't help it. I give him a shit-eating grin.

"Fuck." He blows out a breath and stares at the ceiling.

"I'll be on my best behavior."

I'll apologize. And I'll find out what makes Hayley who she is.

Because suddenly I have the best idea for a book I've had in a long time.

# CHAPTER 4

## HAYLEY

"*H*e really is a nice guy."

At this point I'm not sure if Jade is trying to convince me of my douchebag's neighbor's true character or herself.

"If I consider his arrogant, playboy attitude when we first got there and the way he scared Maisie, I'm having a hard time finding the nice guy you and Shep have been raving about for the last thirty minutes."

While Declan lounges at the picnic table absorbed in his screen and Maisie and Teddy run around the backyard, Shep is manning the grill. Jade and I are in the kitchen putting finishing touches on the sides to go with dinner.

"He is a bit…flirtatious."

I huff a laugh. "That's the understatement of the year. The man essentially drooled all over my shoes the first time he met me, and the next, he acted like a wounded, hibernating grizzly."

She shrugs. "He works late at the bar sometimes—"

"Oh." This huff is full of a lot less humor. "Of course he works at a bar."

"Actually, Hayls, he kind of owns the bar. Well, not kind of, he does. He bought it a few years ago. It was a total dive, but he fixed it up. It's called Expedition Brewing. Have you been there yet?"

Shit. My stomach sinks. I planned to take the kids there for dinner one night this week. Not anymore. Because my plans also include avoiding Mr. Tall, Handsome, and Grumpy until the wedding. We leave the day after, so I can put up with him for one day.

"No, and we're not going to either," I tell her.

"Hayley—"

She's cut off by the sound of the doorbell.

Jade is elbow deep in potato salad so she sends a pleading look my way. "Would you mind grabbing that?"

"Me?" With a sigh, I set down the bag of chips I was opening.

As soon as I open the door, I want to wring my friend's neck. Because standing on the other side is a six-foot-something-sized irritation wrapped in a tempting package.

"What are you doing here?" I grit out, tightening my hold on the doorknob. Just the sight of him makes me want to smack him in the face with the solid wood.

Peeling off the aviators he's wearing as a defense against the bright sunshine outside, he sends me a smile. In most universes it would be a kind, polite smile that one person might exchange with another as they got to know each other.

In my world? My panties dampen and my core throbs.

In other words, it might be time for me to check myself into a mental institution because I've obviously gone insane.

"Hayley."

The timbre of his voice as his lips wrap around my name sends a shiver down my spine.

Rob and I were together for almost twelve years, yet nothing he said ever made desire shimmer in electric currents through my body the way that one word does. Or maybe it's an aneurysm. Or a stroke. There has to be a reasonable explanation for these sensations.

*Get a hold of yourself. This asshole made your baby cry. You are not attracted to him.*

The memory of Maisie's tears helps clear away the hypnotic trance I've fallen into, and with a shake of my head, I take a deep breath.

"Why are you following me?"

"Following you?" He scoffs and steps around me into the house like he belongs here.

"Why else are you here?" I hiss, careful to keep my voice quiet so Jade doesn't hear.

"Jade and Shep invited me."

"*What?*" My screech echoes through the room. So much for not drawing attention.

"Hayls, you okay out there? Who was it?" Jade calls from the kitchen.

Jagger brings a long finger to his lips. To that damn plump flesh beneath it. His top lip is just a little bigger than the bottom, the softness a contradiction to the rest of the man. What would it be like to kiss him?

Stroke. I'm having a stroke. It's the only explanation for my ridiculous thoughts.

"It's just me," Jagger calls out to Jade, taking a step closer to me.

"I wouldn't usually foist myself on you, but I wanted the chance to apologize for my behavior when you came to town. I've been…distracted. And I let that make me more irritable than usual."

Apprehension mixed with curiosity stir in my stomach. "If you wanted to apologize, why didn't you just come by the house?"

"Would you have answered the door?"

"Yes," I say instantly, but I stumble over my words as he arches one of those dark brows. "No. Probably not anyway."

The half smile he gives me is more lethal than the full-wattage version.

"I figured. But I wanted to apologize. I'm sorry."

He holds out a hand and his gaze locks with mine.

"Truce?" he asks.

The angry part of me wants to stay mad, to hate Jagger Brooks with everything I have. But the other part—the woman I once was mixed with the tired mom I've become—doesn't want to keep hating someone so intent on apologizing. It takes a lot of energy to hate.

I slip my palm into his, and an electric arc shoots through my body. I have to bite back a gasp, so my voice is strangled when I respond. "T-truce."

"Can we start over?"

"Start over?" God, I'm parroting him like a damn bird. I yank my hand free of his grasp in hopes that the disconnection restores my faculties.

"I'm Jagger. I live near Teal Lake and I own Expedition Brewing in town."

"Hayley. I'm from Colorado Springs. I'm here visiting my best friend and I'm going to be the maid of honor in her wedding in a few weeks."

"Well, Hayley No Last Name. I'm going to be your best man. Well, I'll be *Shep's* best man, but I'm at your disposal too. For anything."

"Fuller. My last name is Fuller."

He tilts his head to one side and assesses me. "Hayley Fuller."

"Yeah," I say, the single word a little too breathy.

"Oh, hey, Jagger." Jade joins us from the kitchen.

The bubble we've been wrapped in since Jagger got here disappears, and reality washes over me. I take a deep breath and put some distance between myself and my sexy neighbor.

"Shep's out by the table. You got here just in time. Food is ready," she says, wiping her hands on a towel as she sidles up beside me.

"Sorry, I'd have been here sooner but I needed to stop at the bar. POS system went down. But I come bearing gifts." He holds up a six-pack of beer. "My peach pale ale."

"With the Palisade peaches?" Jade asks.

I can almost see the drool from here.

"Duh. First batch to the happy couple."

"Oh my God, Hayley, you have to try this." She grasps my hand and tugs me into the backyard.

I look over my shoulder to find Jagger following us like an obedient puppy.

Maisie spots him almost immediately and stops in the middle of the yard while Teddy runs circles around her feet.

"Mais—" I start toward her, but Jagger speaks up behind me.

"There's the other young lady I owe my apology too."

He sets the six-pack on the outdoor table, then approaches her slowly, rubbing his hands on the front of his jeans. I follow behind until I'm close enough to make out his words when he crouches next to my daughter.

"Hi, Maisie."

She ducks her chin and turns away just slightly. "Hi."

"I'm sorry for scaring you about the bear."

"I'm not scared." She puts on a brave face, but she can't hide the slight tremble of her bottom lip. Tomboy she might be, but she's still five.

Jagger chuckles.

"That might be the case, but I still shouldn't have been mean. I'm sorry."

He looks back at me and I nod encouragingly.

"I have a present for you."

My heart stutters just a little. He bought her a present?

"You did?" Her eyes widen and instantly sparkle.

"I did." He reaches into his back pocket and pulls out a small vial on a woven lanyard.

"What is it?" she asks, taking it from him gently.

"That's the fun part. I stopped at one of the stores in town and picked that up for you. It's Bear B Gone."

"Bear B Gone?" she echoes, holding the vial closer and studying the label.

I move closer, and sure enough there's a bear with a red circle and line through it on the label.

Pressing my lips together, I study him. As Teddy sniffs at the vial, distracting Maisie, Jagger mouths that he'll explain in a minute. With a nod, I take a step back and let him finish with Maisie.

"It has this string so you can wear it around your neck."

She holds it out to him. "Can you help?"

"Er...sure." He unwinds the lanyard and loops it over her neck.

"Thank you." She holds her arms out and throws herself at him with such force he has to drop a hand to the ground for balance to absorb her hug.

"What did I tell you?" Jade murmurs in my ear.

"Yeah, okay, he's a pretty nice guy."

"Who's a nice guy?" Shep asks, embracing Jade from behind.

"Jagger," Jade explains as she snuggles against her fiancé.

"Jagger what?" Jagger asks, popping up and joining us. Maisie has already abandoned him to show Declan her gift.

"Nothing," I answer quickly. "What's in that bottle?"

"A little peppermint, lavender, and lemon oil. It's safe," he assures me.

"I trust you." The words are out before I realize what I'm saying.

He studies me as if he, too, questions the words.

"With this," I add. "She seems to enjoy it."

Declan doesn't look up from his phone when Maisie

approaches, so with a shrug, she takes off and spins around the yard while Teddy lies under a tree watching her.

"Thank you," I tell him.

He dips his chin. "Anytime."

We've only interacted for a handful of minutes since the kids and I came to town, but already, this man confuses me. And though I wasn't lying when I told him I trusted his judgment with the Bear B Gone for Maisie, I don't trust the level of chaos he's incited with his earlier behavior followed by this nice guy routine. Rob could be charming when he screwed up too. Look where that got me.

I can be polite to Jagger. He's the best man in my best friend's wedding. We're neighbors. Spending time together is inevitable.

But that doesn't make us friends.

He asked for a truce.

Polite neighbor is a truce.

Co-participant in the wedding party is a truce.

But that's all that will exist between Jagger Brooks and me.

Even if my daughter is now looking at him like he hung the moon.

# CHAPTER 5

## JAGGER

"'*W*riting is ten percent typing and ninety percent staring at your computer trying to find a better way to describe a piece of toast.' Well, fuck you too, social media."

With a sigh, I click out of the browser window. This is what I get for ignoring my blank document to scroll social media in hopes that it would inspire words. But no. The words are just as stuck as they were an hour ago. They haven't magically written themselves—they never do. They've also never been this elusive. But every time the cursor hypnotizes me with its rhythmic blinking, visions of warm brown eyes and a soft smile infiltrate my thoughts. The look I caught on Hayley's face when I walked over to apologize to Maisie last night.

"Focus, dipshit."

I shake my head to clear the images that have haunted me since I left Jade and Shep's last night. They came to me in my dreams, and into the several hours I attempted to write this morning.

The damn cursor hasn't moved one character.

And Hayley's face still swims to the surface of the bright white document.

"Fuck," I groan and scrub my hands down my face.

My phone vibrates next to me, snagging my attention.

BRITT

How goes the book?

My younger sister, Brittany, is the only one who knows my secret. Fuck, her weekend in Vegas eight years ago is what I based my first book on. The truth made for some good inspiration. Who else would believe that my kid sister spent a wild weekend in Vegas with a rock star?

It's not.

Got any new stories for me? Maybe that'll prompt something.

Ha! No. My life has provided enough fodder for your pornos.

I grind my teeth and bite back a growl. She fucking *knows* this pushes my buttons.

Keep it up, brat, and you won't get the next book early.

I thought nothing was written yet?

Bye, Britt.

Wait!

I wasn't texting you just to give you shit.

That would be a first.

::tongue sticking out emoji::

Word is you have a new neighbor.

With a huff, I drop my head and pinch my brow.

> How the fuck did you hear that?

Um, need I remind you that the small-town
gossip wheel is what prompted my move to
Denver?

I can't hold back the sigh as I read her text. The gossip is the worst part about living in a small town. But where I can ignore all the talk about me and my involvement with tourists, Britt got sick of being painted with the same brush, but not the same judgment.

Double fucking standards at their finest.

> A new neighbor isn't unusual. People are always
> coming and going from next door.

I heard she's pretty.

She's gorgeous. Not that I'll share that opinion with my baby sister.

> She's okay I guess.

You're no fun.

> Oh well.
>
> Shouldn't you be at work anyway?

Shouldn't you?

I'm not due at the bar for another few hours. I set my alarm for the ungodly hour of six so I'd have plenty of quiet time to bang out a chapter. Maybe two.

Instead the words aren't coming and I'm getting shit talked by my sister. Good times.

> I have a few hours. Hopefully I can finish this chapter first.

Well, what are you waiting for?

> Someone is bothering me.

Love you too, bro.

Text me later.I want details on the neighbor. First bit of excitement I've heard from up there in a while.

> How did you even hear about her?

I have my sources.

> Whatever. You can see her yourself. You're still coming to Jade and Shep's wedding, right?

If I can get the time off.

Britt's job is constantly fucking up her plans. Her boss is a total dick, and I've threatened to talk to him on multiple occasions. But every time I do, Britt threatens to kick my ass. She may be younger than me by two years, but the girl has some serious fighting skills courtesy of having to deal with an older brother and the three years of jiu jitsu she took in middle school.

> Why don't you quit and move back here? Come work at the bar.

Pass.

But thanks for the offer.

Gotta go. TTYL.

> Bye.

I toss my phone on the desk and lean back in my chair,

focusing on the little black blinking line. It took a month to write my first book. My latest book took two weeks. I'm pushing past the three-month mark with this one.

The reasonably quiet morning should have helped me get some words knocked out. Outside of Britt's texts, there have been no distractions. Not even a sound from the rambunctious crew next door.

It's fine. My plan is to ignore my new neighbor, her kids, and the dog. I have the capacity to ignore. I've done it before.

Instead, it's too quiet, and my thoughts are too loud in the overwhelming silence. My brain isn't focused on the book I need to write, but on the sexy mom next door. Pushing thoughts of her from my mind once again, I snag my coffee cup from my desk and lift it to my mouth only to discover the damn thing has betrayed me. All the life-giving nectar of caffeine is gone. Has been for a while based on the brown ring dried on the bottom of the mug.

"Good thing I can make another pot," I grumble and stand from my desk.

I'm at the bottom of the stairs when a scream penetrates the solid wooden door.

No, not a scream.

Crying.

"What the…?"

I sling open the door, step out onto the front porch, and scan the area, looking for the source. The crying is louder now, and it's coming from around the back of my house. I set the coffee cup on the porch, then jog around the side of the house.

Maisie is on the ground, tears streaming down her face while Teddy sits beside her, concern evident in his posture. He wags his tail once when he spots me, then turns back to his person.

I approach the two of them slowly. "Hey, Maisie, what happened?" Kneeling beside her, I push Teddy's wet black nose out of my field of vision.

"*Oww!*" she wails, pointing to her knee.

An angry red scrape oozes blood. There isn't much, but it looks painful, nonetheless.

"What happened?"

"I want Mommy!"

I peer over my shoulder, hoping she's already headed our way. But there's no sign of Hayley. Though given where Maisie is, I'm not surprised.

"Okay, let's go get her." I angle in closer, ready to help her up. It's only then that I realize a nylon leash is wrapped around Maisie's legs. One end rests on the grass beside her, and the other is still clipped to Teddy's collar.

"Did you trip over Teddy's leash?"

I grasp the looped end and get to work gently untangling the little girl from the nylon.

With her brown eyes fixed on me while tears continue to travel down her cheeks, she nods. "Uh-huh. Mommy said he needs it."

Guilt squeezes my stomach into a knot. I'm the one who told Hayley the dog needed to be on a leash. We're far enough from the main road that he'd be fine without it if not for my complaint.

I secure the leash around my wrist, then slide one arm under her knees and the other around her shoulders. "Okay, gorgeous, let's get you to your mama."

She loops her arms around my neck and clings tightly, her head resting against my chest. The strawberry smell of her shampoo tickles my nose and tightens the guilt. If not for me, she wouldn't be hurt.

"What about Teddy?" Her words are muffled against my shirt.

"I've got him too."

Quickly, I eat up the distance between where I found Maisie and the house. I don't bother to knock. Turning to one side, I manage to twist the knob without setting Maisie down, then make my way inside.

"Maisie, break— What happened?" Hayley slaps a hand to her chest and rushes to us.

Her words break the dam and Maisie's tears return with a vengeance.

"Mommy!" She reaches for Hayley just as Hayley reaches for her and I relinquish the slight weight.

The loss is immediate. The comforting heat of the little girl evaporates in an instant, leaving me feeling strangely bereft.

"She got tangled up in Teddy's leash. Her knee…" I follow Hayley and Maisie into the kitchen.

Teddy and I are silent observers as Hayley settles Maisie on the counter and presses a paper napkin to her knee. She doesn't turn away from her daughter as she grabs a pack of Band-Aids and a small tube of cream from a first aid kit on the counter.

It's awkward—watching the two of them and at a loss as to how I can help. I shift my weight from one foot to the other, brushing my hands down my jeans, racking my brain for the best way to excuse myself. I may have barged in here without knocking, but leaving without making sure Maisie is okay doesn't feel right.

"Ready?" Hayley asks.

"Nooo." Maisie shakes her head, her tangled dark brown hair billowing around her with the effort. Her little fingers grip the rough cloth against her knee.

"It'll make it feel better."

"It'll hurt!" she counters, her sweet little face red and blotchy.

Hayley's sigh is soft, full of patience. "Close your eyes."

The persuasive tone has my own eyes drifting shut. Unlike Maisie, mine pop open after a breath. Maisie's face is scrunched with the effort of keeping her eyes closed, but her grip loosens before it falls away entirely, leaving the scrape on her knee.

"I'm going to tell you a story about a little princess." With expert precision and without making a sound, Hayley opens the wrapper.

"Am I the little princess?"

Hayley scoffs. "Of course! Who else would my little princess be?"

I'm mesmerized by the cadence of her voice. So much so that I don't hear the story. I'm too fixated on the gentle rise and fall of her voice, the way her fingers smooth the cream against the scrape before they softly cover Maisie's injury with the bandage.

Sunlight filters through the kitchen window and paints mother and daughter in a golden halo. Descriptions filter through my blood, settling in my fingers and itching to come out for the first time in weeks.

"Open your eyes," Hayley whispers.

Long eyelashes flutter along the little girl's flushed cheeks before she opens them. Her dark brown eyes are watery, but the tears are no longer falling. She sniffles as she takes in Hayley, who points to the injured knee.

"All better?" Hayley asks.

The smile is back on Maisie's face when she lifts her head from inspecting the bandage. "It's princesses!"

Twin dimples bracket her mouth, as if the tears from moments ago were nothing but a bad dream. It's like the sun has come back out.

It's a punch to the stomach. The need to help her. The need to watch the smile light up the world again. It catches me off guard.

Even more?

I don't hate the sensation as much as I thought I would.

*Wasn't the plan to ignore them?*

Character voices fill my head, demanding to be set free and override the question I don't have an answer to.

Maisie wiggles her way off the counter with help from her mom, and Teddy squirms toward her until I relinquish the leash.

"I...uh...I need to go."

With that, I turn and head for the door. For the first time in a long time, my laptop is calling my name.

# CHAPTER 6

## HAYLEY

*I*t's quiet. Finally.

But almost too quiet.

*Make up your mind.*

A thousand times a day I wish for less noise. Fewer demands for my attention, less arguing between Declan and Maisie…just less. But now? I'm not sure what to do with the silence.

Maisie fell asleep in a camp chair hours ago, chocolate and marshmallow ringing her mouth while her head drooped to one side. The second the s'mores supplies were gone, Declan left our little makeshift campout and went inside, heading straight for his phone and whatever gaming video caught his attention. At least I had a little time with him where he wasn't the sullen tween he's become recently.

Not long ago, he'd have sat in my lap until he fell asleep. Now it's a nightly battle to get him to put his device down and go to bed. I find his window in the house and breathe a sigh of relief when there's no light still burning brightly. He's asleep.

Turning my attention back to the dying fire, I rub at the ache in my chest. My heart hurts for my little boy. The one who wore cartoon characters on his T-shirts and denim overalls. The one

43

with the bright eyes and quick smile that looked so much like Maisie's. But every time his dad ignores him, the light dims a little more.

"Damn you, Rob," I mutter into the silence.

I'd carried Maisie in and wiped her hands and face as best as I could before tucking her in for the night, then I had returned to our little outdoor setup. The fire is almost out, but a crackle of energy runs under my skin. Sleep isn't coming for a while. I lean back in the worn Adirondack chair and shift my attention to the dark house that belongs to Jagger.

What the hell kind of name is Jagger?

Who am I kidding? It fits him perfectly. It fits the dark brown eyes that hold an intensity that's as disconcerting as it is attractive. I could easily devote hours to studying them, watching how the light shifts with the changes of his facial expressions. The smile semi-hidden by the well-trimmed beard.

My palms tingle at the thought of touching the scruff. Rob was always clean-shaven, and there hasn't been anyone else to compare him to—before or after.

*Or during, like Rob.*

"You're not going to find out. You have two kids to focus on and he obviously isn't a kid kind of person."

Only, based on our interaction earlier, he is.

He cradled Maisie in his arms so gently as he came into the house. And his face was etched with such genuine concern while he stood in the kitchen uncertain about what to do. It's another piece in the jigsaw puzzle that's gradually moving the pendulum from hatred of a cocky playboy to liking the man I would bet very few people see.

The way he fidgeted as he watched Maisie and me in the kitchen makes it obvious that he isn't often at a loss for what to do or what to say.

Whereas that's my reality every day. Kids don't come with owner's manuals.

Slamming my eyes shut, I block out the image of the dark house that reminds me of its owner. I lift my chin and slide deeper into the chair, then open my eyes again to take in the blanket of stars above me.

"I'm not interested in Jagger. In dating in general," I tell the dark blue sky.

It won't call me out for being a liar.

My divorce has been final for six months, even though Rob and I separated three months before that. Single woman or not, I have no interest in the opposite sex right now.

But I can't deny the pull of attraction I have toward Jagger.

Regardless, I won't act on it. He's not the right person for me —or the kids. When I do decide to date again, it will be a man who's stable, not an undeniable flirt. Someone who wants to interact with the kids. We're a package deal, after all.

But that whole concept will come later. Right now, I'm nowhere near ready, especially for a man like Jagger Brooks. In his case, I'll never be.

The crunch of tires on rock distracts me from my stargazing. Headlights pan across the firepit, then cast shadows over the lake as Jagger turns into his driveway. The engine cuts off and the sounds of the car settling take over the quiet.

I can't help but hold my breath. Though I'm not sure whether I'm holding it in hopes that he saw me or whether I'm hoping I can remain hidden. My heartbeat kicks up, thundering in my ears as I wait for the car door to open.

Arms wrapped around myself, I watch, wait. My palms are clammy where I'm gripping my upper arms. I don't have to wait long for him to turn in my direction and saunter toward me, all swagger.

I should hate it.

I could walk away.

But I don't hate it. And I'm frozen in place.

"You're up late." His voice is low, husky.

I shrug and motion to the now smoldering firepit. "Waiting for that to die out."

"Aww, and here I thought you were waiting up for me."

A smile twitches at my lips. Though I fight it, it's pointless. Then I'm laughing at his foolish grin. "Has anyone ever told you you're cocky?"

His smile widens and I want to groan. I should have chosen a different word.

"I've heard that a time or two." He winks, but otherwise doesn't add any other innuendo.

I clear my throat and redirect the conversation, steering us back to safer territory. "Are you just getting off work?"

At the same time, he asks, "How's Maisie?"

He drags a hand through his hair and cups the back of his neck. The move leaves his hair, that I've yet to see out of place, mussed. One lock falls forward, making my fingers itch to move it back into place.

"Want to sit?" I ask.

With a nod, he grabs the Adirondack that Declan occupied earlier. He sits with a long sigh, and his cologne surrounds me.

"Maisie's fine," I say. "Once the Band-Aid was in place, she perked right up."

"That's good."

My heart expands in my chest at the thought of my little girl. "One thing I've learned as a mom? There's not much that can't be fixed with Band-Aids and ice packs."

One corner of his mouth kicks up. "Oddly enough, that makes sense."

"One of the secrets of parenting."

He plants his forearms on the armrests of his chair and leans back. "I'll take your word for it."

"What about you?" I ask.

"What about me?" It's dark, but not too dark to make out the way he lifts one brow.

"Just getting off work?"

"Yep." He nods. "The place was dead, so I closed up early. How did you know I worked at night?"

Heat flushes my chest. "I…um…I asked Jade."

The Cheshire-cat grin he gives me makes the heat creep up into my cheeks. "Oh, you did, did you?"

With a huff, I roll my eyes. "Not like that. I wanted to make sure the kids didn't bother you. I know Maisie can be a bit…"

He tilts forward and squeezes my knee gently. The warmth travels up my leg and settles in my core. One part of me wants to recoil while the other part keeps me where I am.

"Maisie's fine. I'm sorry I was a grouchy asshole that first day. I was in a bad mood, and I took it out on you and her both."

"Bad mood about what?" I tilt my head to one side. "Anything I can help with?"

His fingers twitch against the inside of my leg before he pulls away. *No, dammit, I enjoyed that touch.*

"I'll figure it out. What did Jade tell you about me?"

Ah. The classic subject change. Obviously, he doesn't want to talk about what's bothering him.

"That you own the bar in town."

"Technically, it's a microbrewery, but it is easier to just call it a bar," he corrects.

"I should probably know the difference since I grew up in Colorado, huh?"

He shrugs. "I don't think many people care. It was a bar before I bought it, though. A dive bar at that."

"What made you change it?"

"I always liked the concept of making my own beer. And I liked the idea of a place that would appeal to the locals as well as tourists looking for a place to hang out when they're done skiing."

"How long have you owned it?"

"Why are all these questions about me? How about I ask a few about you?"

With a shrug, I duck my chin. I'm not sure I want to get into details about myself and my past. Not tonight. "There's not much to tell about me."

He taps my foot with the toe of his boot. "How about I be the judge of that?"

I take a deep breath and sigh it out. "I'm a former stay-at-home mom turned tutor."

"Jade said you met in college."

"You asked Jade about me?"

Unlike me, he isn't embarrassed by being found out. No, he gives me a mischievous grin when I call him on it. "I was curious. Sue me."

With my lips pressed together, I tip my head in a *yeah, right* look.

"There's nothing to be curious about. Yes. I met Jade in college. I dropped out when I got pregnant with Declan. Rob had graduated already and took a job in Colorado Springs, so we got married and moved there. Maisie came a few years later."

"And the divorce?"

Startled by the forward question, I sit up straighter. When I force myself to look at him, his expression is filled with a genuineness that surprises me and the flippant answer I am about to give dies on my lips.

"Rob was never interested in being married or having kids. Come to find out, his parents forced him to 'do the right thing' when I got pregnant. Told him if he didn't, he'd be cut off from his inheritance. Though in his eyes, doing the right thing didn't include being faithful. So he cheated. A lot." The ache in my stomach that I thought had mostly disappeared after our divorce was final returns at the memories that hit me. "I put up with it for way too long. The final straw came when I found out he'd been in a two-year relationship with one of his coworkers."

Jagger's jaw drops. "Holy shit."

"Yep." I nod, shoulders sagging. "I didn't want to be that woman anymore. Declan is old enough to understand more than I'd like when it comes to that. I knew then that if I didn't end it, then he'd think that what I allowed was okay."

"So you asked for the divorce?"

"Yeah. Not like he fought it. He didn't ask for anything except his personal stuff. Not the house or the car. Not even the kids. He never brought them up once."

"What?" He lunges forward in his seat, looking as shocked as I felt when I came to that realization.

"He pays child support. And alimony. He told the judge he wanted two weekends a month, but he's yet to take them overnight. Saw them once for a few hours right after the divorce. Called Declan on his birthday a few months ago. Forgot Maisie's. And other than the monthly payments, we haven't heard from him since."

"What an asshole."

"Jade and I have called him a lot worse."

"Good girl."

Oh, Jesus, that phrase, whispered huskily between the two of us, should not make me hot and bothered. I probably need to cool it with the reading for a while.

I squirm in my seat and try to ignore the heat that crawls through my body. "So that's enough of my sob story."

He frowns and laces his fingers in front of him, arms still planted on the armrests. "Why do you think it's a sob story?"

"Why shouldn't I?"

"The way I see it, you're a strong woman who puts her kids first, regardless of what their douchebag of a dad does. He's not worth their time. Or yours. You're showing them how to value themselves rather than let other people bring them down. You're fucking awesome."

Warmth tingles through me for a third time now. First

embarrassment, then attraction. Now? I don't know how to describe it. Comfort? Delight? Regardless, my emotions have been all over the place in the span of a fifteen-minute conversation. Maybe it's time for bed after all.

"Thank you." I let out a long breath. "I guess I should probably let you get home. Looks like the fire's out."

I stand and he follows, then takes a step to close the small distance between us.

"I meant what I said." His dark eyes lock with mine, and he lifts a hand to cup my chin.

Like I could look away if I wanted to. Instead I'm stuck, too paralyzed to move.

"You're amazing." The words are only a whisper.

I slick my tongue over my suddenly dry lips, and he tracks the movement.

"Hayley."

A shiver runs down my body at the way he says my name.

"Hmm?"

"How long has it been since you were kissed?"

My heart trips over itself. "A while."

And even then, it was more for show at one of Rob's work parties.

"I want to kiss you," he admits.

"We shouldn't," I tell him, garnering the modicum of willpower I possess.

He's not the type of person I need to get involved with.

"Do you always do what you should?"

"Yes." The word is a breath into the warm night and scatters between the stars.

At this point, I really wish I didn't.

He leans back and swallows thickly, and just like that, the dreamlike bubble that surrounds us fades.

"I'm sorry." His words are loud in the silence.

I take a small step back. "You don't need to apologize."

"I feel like I should. Again."

"It's fine." I don't want him to kiss me. Even if my lips still tingle with anticipation.

"I'm not apologizing for wanting to, Hayley."

"Then why are you apologizing?"

He roughs a hand along his jaw. "I wish I fucking knew."

"Well, let me know if you figure it out." I take another step back, then I turn for the house.

He grasps my wrist before I get too far. "Fuck it," he mumbles.

The words are narrowly past his lips when his mouth covers mine. My eyes drift closed, and I have to grip his arms for balance as the universe tips on its axis and shooting stars spark behind my closed eyelids. And that's before he licks along the seam of my lips. I open obediently, and his tongue gently explores my mouth, teasing me until my own joins in the dance.

Never.

I've never been kissed like this.

This is what all the books I read talk about. A chemistry I thought was purely fiction. This kiss has my entire body craving more. That hand is cupping my jaw again, and with slight pressure, he tilts my head and deepens the kiss. The rest of the world fades into a blur in the background. All I want is to keep kissing him. His other hand settles on the small of my back and tucks me into his body so close that the proof of his arousal presses between us.

Fuck, yes.

He gentles his movements, then peppers me with several chaste kisses before he breaks the connection. I blink my eyes open to find him staring at me. A sheen of moisture coats his lips.

"You're beautiful," he murmurs. "And I want more."

His words echo my own thoughts.

Yes, more. More of these drugging kisses. More of the fire that sizzles in my blood and the tightening in my core. Definitely more.

"But I don't want to rush this. You deserve more."

There's that word again.

"You deserve to be savored."

He leans down and presses a kiss to my forehead.

"Goodnight, Hayley."

Inside me, disappointment wars with the admiration. I want more now. But I also need to think about this rather than relying on my barely awake libido.

"Goodnight."

"I'd walk you to your door, but then I might not be able to stop from asking for more now."

My heart stutters in my chest. Damn. He's like a book boyfriend come to life with lines like that.

"O-okay."

He stays where he is, shoving his hands into his pockets.

After a heartbeat, I turn and head for my porch.

"And Hayley?"

I turn around to find him standing in the same spot.

"Yeah?"

"I meant what I said."

The hunger in his eyes answers my question.

Savor.

My core pulses at the phantom pressure of his lips on mine.

"You won't get any complaints from me," I tell him with a wink. "Goodnight, Jagger."

His low groan follows me into the house and into dreams filled with heat...and Jagger Brooks.

# CHAPTER 7

## HAYLEY

*I*'m zeroed in on the coffee maker the next morning in the way a cat watches a mouse. The sweet nectar that is the difference between exhaustion and the ability to get through my day can't come fast enough. Dreams of Jagger haunted me all night. More of those drugging kisses. More of the leashed possessiveness of his touch.

Caffeine isn't optional at this point.

It's a necessity if I have any chance of gaining control over my thoughts again. They haven't been my own since the moment Jagger's mouth connected with mine.

The slow drip into the pot has just finished when a soft knock interrupts my memories. It's as if my focus on the man has conjured him, because when I turn, he's standing on the other side of the door, clearly visible through the window cutout. His dark hair is wet and slicked back from a face shadowed with stubble I traced with my fingers last night.

When he knocks again, I shake free of my stupor. I take the few steps to the door, and with a fortifying breath, I open it and silently motion him inside while praying that Teddy doesn't hear the noise and tear through the house to check out the visitor, barking the whole way. My plan was to enjoy my coffee before the kids woke up.

"Good morning, beautiful."

I huff a laugh as I glance down at the oversized T-shirt with the stretched-out neck and the sleep boxers that I consider pajamas. I've also tossed my hair up into a messy bun to get it off my neck.

"You need glasses," I mutter.

One side of his mouth quirks up.

"Had them. For years. Coke-bottle style. Then contacts before I finally got Lasik a few years ago."

I can picture that.

But I can also picture his brown eyes softened by a small pair of glasses. Wire rims. No. Darker. A little thicker. My nipples pucker against my shirt, and I cross my arms to hide my body's reaction to the image.

He moves effortlessly around the kitchen, grabbing two mugs out of the cabinet and pouring coffee into both.

"Cream? Sugar?" he asks and cranes a look over his shoulder at me.

"Just creamer," I tell him.

His moves are graceful as he heads for the refrigerator, pulls my creamer out, and tops one cup off.

With a soft smile, he holds it up to me. "Thank you," I murmur, surprised by how at ease he is in this kitchen.

"Been here often?" I can't help but ask.

Regretting the question instantly, I cringe. I don't want to know the answer. But I can't take it back now that it's out there.

He takes a small drink from his own cup, but his eyes don't leave my face.

"Do you really want to know? I could lie to you, but I don't want to."

Maybe I should be turned off by the implication, but his

honest response catches me off guard. With a small shake of my head, I say, "No, not really," and leave it at that.

With a small nod, he takes another drink, then we fall into silence. I'm not sure about him, but I don't trust myself not to open my mouth without caffeine. I'll say something stupid. Or kiss him again.

And that's a bad idea.

*Isn't it?*

My lips don't seem to think so. They tingle with the desire to brush against his again.

"Where are the kids?" he asks, thankfully interrupting my memory of our kiss last night.

I huff a laugh. "Asleep still, thank God."

I set my cup down and perch on the counter next to it.

His attention strays to my legs before moving slowly back to my face.

"I bet that doesn't happen very often."

"Once in a blue moon or two."

Teddy races into the kitchen then, thankfully without barking even if the sound of his paws on the floor resembles a stampede of elephants.

Kneeling, Jagger rubs his hands along Teddy's head and back until the dog flops to his side and rolls to his back. Jagger chuckles and rubs the puppy's belly, making one leg bounce uncontrollably. A smile bites into my cheeks at the two of them.

Jagger's hands had briefly found my bare skin last night. Calloused, large, warm. I'm jealous of my own dog and the undivided attention this man is giving him. I take several more sips of coffee, letting it work its magic, while I watch the two of them.

Jagger unfolds from the floor, and Teddy follows, popping up and shaking his body, setting his tags tinkling.

"How would you feel about getting the kids up?" He picks up his coffee cup and closes some of the distance between us.

I hold my breath as he gets closer. For what, I'm not sure. But it takes several heartbeats for his question to register.

"I'm sorry?"

"I'd like to take you guys to Misty Lake. Weather is supposed to be perfect for it, and I think you and the kids would enjoy it."

I clutch my warm mug to my chest. "Don't you have to work today?"

Why am I looking for excuses to not spend time with him?

Oh yeah, because I'm not as confident in my self-control as I should be. Because I'm attracted to him and I shouldn't be.

He shakes his head. "Expedition is closed on Mondays."

"And you're sure you want to spend your day off with us?"

He takes another step toward me. Then he sets his coffee cup down and grips the edge of the counter on either side of my hips, caging me in. The way his body heat surrounds me makes me want to loop my hands around his neck and drag his mouth to mine.

"Yes," he murmurs, leaning in.

"Not just me. It'll be the kids too."

We're a package deal.

He nods. "And Teddy."

I rear back, eyes wide. "Teddy?"

"Why do you sound so surprised?" He slips a hand down my hip to my upper thigh and teases the bare skin there, short-circuiting my brain.

I can count on one hand the number of times Rob expressed any interest in spending time as a family.

"The kids, and the dog, and me? Do you know what you're getting yourself into?"

"I know what I'm doing." He lowers his gaze to my mouth but drags it back up again quickly. With a groan, he closes his eyes as if he's in pain.

"What's wrong?" I ask, lifting my free hand to his bicep.

He blinks his eyes open and regards me, wearing a serious expression. "I'm trying really hard not to kiss you right now."

"Okay?"

"My self-control is only so strong. And when you drag your tongue along your lips like that, what I'm hanging on to frays a little further."

I didn't even realize I had done that. But I know exactly what I'm doing when I set my coffee on the counter, hook my feet around his thighs, and pull him closer.

"You're playing with fire, Hayley," he says, his breath mingling with mine.

The way his lips form my name sends heat spreading through my body. "Maybe I am."

"I want to kiss you," he murmurs. His mouth is so close to mine, the movement is pure torture.

"So why don't you?"

His responding groan is so guttural it's practically a growl. "You asked for it."

He claims my mouth, pushing his tongue past the barrier of my lips. I thread my fingers through his hair and hold him against me. His hands flex against my hips, searing me through the sleep shorts I wish would evaporate into thin air.

God, the man can kiss. Last night's kiss absolutely was an anomaly, but only because this morning's is even better. If that one blew every other kiss of my life out of the water, how could it possibly get better?

But it does.

It's the first kiss excitement I read about mingled with antici-pation because I already know how he knows how to master my lips.

He tastes like a mix of toothpaste, coffee, and something uniquely him. Whatever it is, it's intoxicating. Last night wasn't an anomaly. I want more. I need more. And the part that is telling me to slow down is being silenced with every heartbeat that passes with his lips connected to mine.

"Mom! I'm hungry." Maisie's voice reaches the kitchen the second before she does.

Jagger jumps back and separates us by almost a foot, breathing just as heavily as I am. The sudden appearance of a five-year-old cools my libido faster than a bucket of ice water would.

"What, Mais?" I ask, doing my best to unscramble my brain and catch my breath.

Maisie stands in the doorway, hands on her hips and her head tilted in confusion. "Mr. Jagger, what are you doing here?"

"How do you feel about going swimming in a lake that looks like a mirror?" he asks.

Her small frown instantly morphs into the brightest smile. She's bouncing in place when she turns to me. "Can we go, Mommy?"

My attention shifts from the hopeful face of my five-year-old to the heated smolder of the man who created the hope.

"Let's go wake up Declan. Looks like we need to pack for the lake."

⛰ ⛰ ⛰

Misty Lake does in fact resemble a mirror and reflects a gorgeous blue summer sky.

We're barely out of the car when Declan and Teddy take off for the lake.

"Dec, your—"

But I don't need to worry about Declan's shoes or his T-shirt. My gangly almost-teen looks more like a kid Maisie's age again as he strips off his T-shirt and kicks off his shoes just before hitting the water. Teddy beats Declan there by seconds, running through and splashing the water up in a celebration of victory.

He barks happily, already soaked.

A smile curves my lips at the unfiltered joy of the playful behavior in front of me.

Maisie scrambles from her seat and rushes to meet her brother and the dog.

"Can she swim?" Jagger asks.

There's a concern in his tone, and I glance over to see him poised to run after her.

"She's fine. I've had her in swim lessons since she was a toddler. She loves the water."

His body relaxes, a deep sigh escaping him.

"Good."

"You put an awful lot of stuff into this car," I tell him, walking toward the back and opening the hatch.

Camp chairs, two coolers, a bag of towels, and another bag of odds and ends are next to a set of fishing poles and a beat-up tackle box.

"I got this. Why don't you go check out the lake with the kids?" he suggests.

"You're sure?"

"I wouldn't have said so if I didn't mean it. Go relax." He nods toward the lake and shoulders two of the bags.

"If you're sure…"

"Go." The way he arches one dark eyebrow and a smirk hovers on his lips makes me want to lean forward and kiss him.

Either that or defy him and see what happens.

That dare simmers in his brown eyes and spreads an equal heat through my body.

But is this more of the playboy coming out to flirt?

I may have kissed him—twice—but for all intents and purposes, he's still a stranger.

My friends may have vouched for him, but was that enough for me? Swallowing the need that continues to build with every breath, I leave him at the car and walk the short trail to the beachy area of the lake.

"Hi, Mommy!" Maisie waves at me before diving back under the water.

Teddy swims back to the shore and gets out, shaking off next to me. I squeal and take several steps to the side.

"Teddy!"

Water droplets now dot my T-shirt and shorts. He takes my retreat as a game of chase and bounds over to jump and put his paws on my midsection.

"You're wild, dog," I tell him and push him down.

"Mommy, come play." Maisie pops back above the surface.

"Baby, how about you come get sunscreen on? You too, Declan!" I raise my voice to get his attention farther out in the lake.

He starts back and Maisie does as well.

Turning around, I find one of the bags Jagger has dropped off with a bottle of sunscreen poking out.

In the time it takes me to sunscreen Maisie and supervise Declan—and continue to push Teddy out of the way of licking it —Jagger has unpacked the car and set up the camp chairs.

"You want to go check out the water?" Jagger asks and steps behind me.

He's not touching me, but the heat of his body in the sun reaches out and wraps around me. I want to lean back against him. I want to give in to the electricity that arcs between us and pulls me toward him.

*Girl, you need to cool off.*

My libido is getting the better of me. And the last time that happened, I ended up pregnant and married.

Maybe the water is what I need to help douse the flames that just being close to him is creating.

"Is it cold?" I turn around, glad for my sunglasses that are in place since he's stripped off his T-shirt when I wasn't paying attention.

It's not the first time I've seen him shirtless—hell, he answered the door in a towel the first day I met him—but the sudden awareness of him since our first kiss last night adds a level of intensity not there before.

How am I supposed to act like I did before the kiss? I can't act on the attraction. Jagger is not the right guy for me to finally break my self-imposed celibacy with. Especially given that my kids are less than fifty feet from the two of us.

This is not "just friends" feelings. This is more like friends with benefits. And I can't do that. But it doesn't stop me from admiring the specimen in front of me.

Deep lines define his chest and abs, and I use my sunglasses as a shield to drag my gaze down his body until my eyes reach the waistband of his swim trunks. He's not a gym bro, but he's fit and toned, the muscles shifting and bunching the result of actual work rather than the cultivated look that Rob liked so much.

*No, that asshole doesn't belong here. Ogle what's in front of you.*

Wow.

My fingers itch with the fierce, but unfamiliar need to reach out and trace the lines. There's a light smattering of chest hair that sprinkles down his chest and disappears into his swim trunks.

"You should stop looking at me like that," he murmurs.

My eyes fly to his face.

"You may be wearing sunglasses, Hayley, but you have another tell." He reaches over and drags his finger along my lip that's currently caught between my teeth.

I release my bite, blowing a breath that teases his finger.

"Do you need sunscreen?" He pulls the bottle from my clenched fingers and chuckles. "Glad the lid didn't pop off as hard as you're squeezing."

That deep rumble has a direct connection to my core, and I

squeeze my legs together and fight the whimper that builds in my throat. I can almost imagine his hands on my body, rubbing slowly along the skin and igniting every nerve in his wake.

If he touches me, I may just spontaneously combust with the heat that's already building between us.

"Ummm…"

I should say no. But my lips can't form the word.

"Turn around."

He says the two words with such confidence, such swagger, I'm doing what he said before I fully process it.

The bottle clicks open and I suck in a breath in anticipation of that first touch.

*Please.*

"Do you want to take your tank top off?"

Getting my head out of the gutter, I realize my tank top over my one piece won't prevent him from reaching the areas he needs. It also provides a welcome camouflage to my stiff nipples that poke against the front of my suit.

"It's okay," I assure him while simultaneously trying to assure myself.

He starts slowly, sweeping my arms with the lotion until it's rubbed in and then lifting his hands to my shoulders.

I moan at the way he kneads the tight muscles and flush at the loud sound. He doesn't say anything but continues until every area of exposed skin is covered with the protective lotion.

"All done."

I should use the moment to put some much needed distance between us. My libido has other ideas.

"Your turn?" My voice is husky, and I swallow in an attempt to clear my throat.

He steps in front of me, and I sink my teeth into my lower lip. This man is my own personal Greek god come to life. His broad shoulders taper down to a narrow waist, and I move closer and suck in the scent of soap and cologne. Bergamot and sandalwood and something uniquely him. The sun-kissed bronze of his skin calls to my fingers like a homing beacon.

*Stop standing here like an idiot.*

Opening the bottle, I squirt some lotion into my hands and lift them to a safe space to touch—his shoulder blades.

"You spend a lot of time out here?" I ask, biting back a giggle when he shivers at the first contact of the lotion against his warm back.

"Some. Usually I just hang out at home."

"We could have stayed there. You live next to a lake."

"We could, but this one is prettier. Figured it would be more fun for you and the kids." His voice is strained, uncomfortable, and I see why when he spins around quickly.

"I wasn't—" I follow his mortified gaze and glance down and see the rigid outline of his dick against his swim trunks. "Oh."

When I avert my eyes, his embarrassment is clear in his ruddy cheeks.

"Yeah. *Oh.* Maybe I better finish," he tells me.

*Finish* finish? It isn't until he holds out a hand for the sunscreen and I reluctantly give it up that I understand his meaning. I'd rather slather the front part of him, too, with all his toned muscles and washboard abs, but based on his reaction to what I've already done, this is probably the safer choice given the close proximity of the kids.

Distance is probably best right now.

"I'm going to go check out the lake," I say.

I wade in slowly, enjoying the sandy bottom of the lake instead of the muck I've experienced before. The water is cool, but not cold, welcome on my overheated skin.

"Hi, Mommy." Maisie swims up next to me and waits for me to wade farther out before reaching for me.

I lift her wet and slippery body into my arms, her cool embrace grounding me, reminding me of who I am and my responsibilities. I can't spend all day with my hands on my sexy neighbor. I'm a mom.

"Hi, baby."

"Hey, Declan, want to go try to fish?" Jagger's shout draws my attention back to the shore.

"Huh?" He looks confused as he doggy-paddles and looks at Jagger.

"Fishing. There's some decent trout fishing down at the bend there." Jagger lifts the two poles and points them a little farther down the beach where the shore curves.

I hold my breath and wait for Declan to consider the invitation. The last time he went fishing was as a toddler with my dad. He looks over to me and I smile and nod.

"It's okay." The words are too quiet for him to hear, but they still seem to reach him.

His face brightens and he turns his attention back to Jagger.

"Um, yeah. Okay, that sounds…cool." He starts to swim back to shore, a smile I haven't witnessed in a while stretching his cheeks.

God, where did this man come from?

He's dangerous…but not just to my libido.

To my heart. To my kids' hearts.

Maisie reaches up and her finger traces the smile on my lips.

"I like this place," she says.

I look down at her little grin.

"You do?"

She nods.

"You smile here."

She's right.

I haven't smiled this much in ages.

But it's not the place.

Instead it's the man currently showing my son the proper way to cast his fishing line in a lake that reflects the perfect day around us.

# CHAPTER 8

## HAYLEY

*H*ours later, I'm guiding a half-asleep Declan to his room while Jagger carries Maisie behind me. Poor Teddy crashed right inside the door, too tired after chasing bugs to do more than collapse on the floor, stretching his body out directly in front of the couch.

I smile at the picture he makes before continuing to guide Declan upstairs to his room.

"Here you go, buddy." I direct him to his bed.

He falls down face first, down for the count the minute his head touches the pillow. I ease off his flip-flops and drop them next to the bed, then step back into the hallway, pulling the door shut behind me.

Jagger waits patiently, my little girl clutched against his chest. She has her arms looped around him and her face buried in his neck. The image creates a puddle in the place where my heart used to be.

"Do you want me to take her?" I whisper and reach for her.

He shakes his head. "Just tell me where she needs to go."

I open the next door and step back so Jagger can deposit her on the bed. We work together to tuck her in. She murmurs nonsense without opening her eyes, nestling her head into her pillow and clutching her stuffed dog to her chest.

We don't talk until we're downstairs and seated next to each other on the love seat while Teddy snores softly from where he's still passed out in front of the couch.

It's the only reason I don't mind sitting next to Jagger.

*Yeah, right.*

"You and Declan were talking for a while." The two of them spent almost an hour next to the shore while I swam with Maisie and supervised her battle with Teddy and his tug-of-war rope.

"He's a good kid." He stretches his arms up with a yawn, revealing a strip of tan skin.

He's been shirtless most of the day, only shrugging his T-shirt back on as the sun started to dip behind the mountain. I should be used to it. But that little glimpse makes my fingers itch to trace the exposed area. To confirm that he's actually here and not some make-believe book boyfriend who only exists in my imagination.

He drops one arm along the top of the love seat, his fingers dragging a trail of gooseflesh behind them until he settles his arm around my shoulders in a move that reminds me of high school first dates.

Smiling, I lean against him and weave my fingers together in my lap to keep them controlled.

"He is. Was. He's...suddenly, I'm a stranger. I rarely get more than two-word responses anymore. I miss my little boy."

He squeezes my shoulders in a comforting gesture. "He's still there. We had a good talk."

"What did you guys talk about?" I shift on the cushion, angling myself so I can see him.

He keeps his arm on my shoulder, twirling the ends of my ponytail with a finger. "He was telling me about wanting to join the football team next year."

I dip my chin. "He wants to try out for eighth grade football."

"It would be good for him. He seems to really like the idea of it anyway."

"He's a fanatic for football." I lower my gaze to my hands in my lap. "Every year. College and professional."

"Knights fan?" Jagger asks, referencing the pro team in Denver.

"Of course." I give him a small smile.

"Is that something he shared with his dad?"

Just the thought of Rob makes me go rigid, and the smile vanishes from my face.

"Fuck, I'm sorry. I didn't mean—"

"It's okay. I know," I say, working to relax the muscles again. "His dad really doesn't care for sports. Declan gets his athletic ability from my side of the family."

"Your side, huh?"

"I played volleyball in high school. Even got a college scholarship. Until…"

"Until you got pregnant?" he guesses.

I nod.

"It was definitely not the plan. But it was what it was. And I have two beautiful kids."

"What was your plan for school?"

"I was an education major like Jade. I wanted to teach elementary school though. When Rob and I got divorced, I went back to work. I never finished my degree, so I started tutoring."

"Doesn't he pay child support?" He roughs a hand through his hair. "Sorry, that might be too personal."

"It's fine. He does. And alimony. But I don't want to be beholden to him. To have my livelihood depend on his reliability to make those payments every month. It's why I'm going back to school in the fall."

"You are?" he asks, a small smile tipping one side of his lips.

"Yeah. I still like the idea of teaching. It would give me a good schedule with the kids too."

Using his thumb and forefinger, he lifts my chin so I'm forced to look at him.

"You're pretty amazing, Hayley Fuller. And so are your kids."

"Th-thank you," I tell him, ducking my chin as heat creeps up my neck and into my cheeks.

He puts two fingers under my chin to stop me, gently forcing me to look at him again. "You're also quite possibly the most positive person I've ever met. You have the right to be bitter about so many things, yet you aren't."

I shrug. "The way I see it, I can move forward and choose happiness, or live in the past and dwell on the negative. I choose to move forward."

He clears his throat and swallows. "Can I tell you something?"

The butterflies in my stomach freeze. Those words don't have a positive connotation for me.

"Okay?" I say the word hesitantly, my palms clammy as I wait for whatever it is he's going to say.

Was today only a happy memory for me? Is the way that I'm feeling after today one-sided?

"I've been dwelling."

"On the negative?" I ask.

He assesses me for a long moment, his dark eyes serious, all-seeing, and a smile twitches the corners of his mouth. "On our kiss from this morning."

The butterflies thaw and are back with a vengeance and flapping their wings with enough force to create a hurricane.

"You have?" The words are mostly for me, but he's close enough to hear.

"I want a repeat."

"A repeat?"

"Do you mind?"

The anticipation of kissing him again alone has turned my brain to mush. All I can do is parrot back to him.

"Mind?"

One corner of his lips twitches in a half smile. "I'm going to take that as a yes."

With that, he cups my cheek and brushes a thumb along my jaw. He leans in until his lips coast along mine, teasing small kisses from one side to the other before he finally settles his mouth firmly to mine. When his tongue dances with mine, I turn my body so I can take the connection deeper, and splay one hand across his chest. We may be pressed together from hip to chest, but it's not enough. Not for the craving he creates. It's never been like this. Not with Rob or anyone else.

Only with the playboy next door.

But I'm going into this with my eyes wide open. Who he is, what this is. I have no illusions. Shifting, I straddle his lap. I'm rewarded when he cradles my jaw with both hands. His fingertips on my skin send a current of electricity through me as he drags them along my cheeks until he buries them in my hair.

The way his hands tangle in the strands is both reverence and ravishment. His hips pulse when I rub against his erection, and my fingernails dig into the soft cloth of his T-shirt. It's the definition of worship and passion in the meeting of our lips and the urgency of our hands.

Humming, he trails open-mouthed kisses along the sensitive skin of my jaw, then nips at my ear.

"Fuck," he growls, gripping my hips to rub me faster against him.

His voice rips through me as much as his touch, centering every sensation in my core. Every kiss, every glide of his fingertips against my skin is *more*. More than I knew existed, more than I'm used to. But it's not enough.

My breath breaks as sensations overwhelm me and leave me tethered to the man holding me so securely. I drop my head back, pressing farther against him, and he lifts his hands to my breasts. Over the fabric of my tank top and bathing suit, he drags his thumbs along my nipples, igniting an inferno that burns my core.

He sinks his teeth into the spot where my neck and shoulder connect and tugs before laving the spot with his tongue.

"Oh my God."

Is that my voice?

All we're doing is making out on the couch, both of us fully clothed, and it's already hotter than any other experience in my life.

He stands, taking me with him. Automatically, my legs lock around his waist and I cling to his shoulders.

"I've got you, baby."

Baby. The nickname isn't offensive. But right now it makes me feel...cherished.

He flexes his fingers into the soft flesh of my ass, pulling a whimper from me. Slowly, he releases me, so I slide down his body an inch at a time. When my feet touch the floor, he keeps an arm locked around my waist to hold me up. It's a good thing, too, since my knees no longer have the strength.

"You're fucking beautiful," he tells me, brushing a finger along my jaw.

"I—thank you." It's so hard not to argue those words. To just accept them.

But the way he stares at me, the way his hands clutch me, the way his lips worship me—everything tells me more than his words.

He genuinely thinks I'm beautiful. He makes me feel beautiful.

He reaches out, teasing the hem of my tank top, a question in his eyes.

"I want to make you feel good," he tells me.

There isn't a doubt in my mind that he could. He's *already* made me feel amazing. I would cry if he stopped now. So I nod and encourage him. "Please."

The moment stretches between us, our breaths mingling and my body honed to every flicker of his fingers against my nylon-covered stomach. He slowly draws the fabric of my shirt up, as if we have all the time in the world. But his patience is belied in the muscle that tics in his jaw. He splays his hands and glides them smoothly over my lycra-encased breasts, pulling a mewl from me. The warmth that spreads through me at the contact is addicting. I press closer, desperate for more, but he keeps his movements even, slow.

"Shhh."

He continues to move, bringing the shirt up and over my head. He tosses it onto the couch next to us, then bends over, brushing teasing kisses along the bathing suit strap on one shoulder, across my collarbone to the other strap.

The anticipation that thrums through my body makes it hard to hold still. I swivel my hips, searching for friction. He steps closer, grasping them and holding me still against his erection. His mouth fastens to mine in a drugging kiss. The rest of the world fades as I thread my fingers through his hair.

He rubs his hands up and down my hips several times before finally easing his way to the snap and zipper of my shorts. He deftly unfastens them but leaves them in place. "Is this okay?"

"*Yes.*" To prove my point, I push the shorts down so they puddle at my feet, then step out of them.

I'm in just my bathing suit—a one piece that covers the areas I want to hide. But there's nowhere to hide from how he looks at me. I don't want to hide.

Not from him.

"You're so sexy." His voice is rough, like he swallowed a handful of gravel, and his eyes smolder with fire.

My heart races and my skin tingles, begging for more, for that next step. For something it doesn't have the right words to describe, but inherently demands.

He smooths his hands along the waist I wish was smaller to hips that have one or two stretch marks. Cupping my ass and squeezing, he pulses his hips against mine. Stars flash behind my eyes and my legs shake. I tighten my grip on his arms just as his fingers dip below the nylon fabric to find the bare skin of my ass.

"Fuck, what is this thing made of? Who designed it? Some rocket scientist at NASA?"

"It's a shape suit," I explain, gasping when he manages to get both hands under the fabric.

"A what?"

"It helps keep everything…where it belongs."

He tugs at my earlobe with his teeth, then moves lower, nipping at the sensitive skin just below my ear. "It's keeping me from where I belong."

With bravery I can only attribute to the lust flowing through me, I lift a hand to one strap and drag it down my arm. Then I do the same on the other side. As my breasts are revealed, he drops his attention to them. Ignoring my ass, he brings his thumbs and forefingers to my nipples and sets to work tugging and pinching until my legs threaten to buckle again. My nipples have never been this sensitive. Or maybe it's just Jagger's touch that's creating lightning arcs of pleasure between my breasts and my pussy.

"Keep going, baby," he tells me, reminding me of what I was doing before he distracted me so thoroughly.

I shimmy the suit over my stomach, tugging and yanking it down past the control point there. Bunching the fabric in my hands, I push the rest of the way and let it drop to my feet.

Self-consciousness threatens to overwhelm me, but I stand still and absorb his heated sweep from my breasts to my toes.

"Fuck me." He groans, sinking his teeth into that soft bottom lip of his.

"Isn't that my line?" I ask.

In response to my quip, he twists one of my nipples a little sharper. I moan and press closer to him as the fire inside me flares.

"You like that, huh?" He repeats the caress. "What about my mouth? Do you want that too, Hayley?"

The way he uses my name is kerosene on the fire. I'm not a random woman that he can call *baby*, and his use of my name reinforces that.

"Yes."

He leans down and closes his mouth over the distended tip of one breast. But instead of bridging the gap, he boosts me into his arms, his lips landing in the valley between my breasts in a chaste kiss.

"Maybe we should go upstairs," I suggest, raking my fingers along his nape.

His hair teases my breasts as he shakes his head. "If I take you upstairs, this stops being about you."

"That's okay," I tell him.

He's already brought me closer to an orgasm than I've been with another person in over six years.

"Tonight is about making you feel good. Only you."

The look in his eyes when he tips his head back and regards me sends a flood of need crashing through my body.

He lays me down on the couch and kneels next to me. Starting at my fingers, he presses kisses along my arm on one side. Then he turns it and presses more on the underside. When he's done, he lifts my arm out of the way so that it rests over one of the sides. I shift my hips against the couch, seeking friction as I wait for his next move. He pulls back, drinking me in. My nipples tighten under his perusal, and a wolfish smile splits his face. Leaning in, he rubs his five o'clock shadow along the sensitive peak, then repeats the caress on my other breast.

"Please," I tell him again, lifting my hips in urgent plea.

I need more.

"Lift your other arm," he gently commands.

I comply, interlacing my fingers above my head.

Only when I've done that does he lower his mouth to my

breast, rubbing his lips against the tip in another teasing caress. He moves from one side to the other until he sucks the peak into his mouth. Fireworks explode behind my eyelids, and I bite my lip to keep from crying out.

He swirls his tongue, orbiting the hard tip, while he moves a hand to the other breast to tug and pinch. Lightning arcs from my breasts to my pussy and my core spasms, throbbing as my clit screams for attention. He sinks his teeth into my nipple, tugging roughly. This time I can't hold back, crying out as he soothes the bite with his tongue.

"Shhh," he reminds me. "You need to be quieter than that if you want more."

Opening my eyes, I find him hovering over my breasts. His hair is mussed from my fingers, and his lips are plump and swollen from our kisses, but the heat of his gaze is undeniable.

"I do want more," I whisper, every inch of my body aching for him.

He drags one hand from my breast down my belly, stopping just above the apex of my thighs. My body quivers, on an edge that only he can soothe, and I part my legs.

Without breaking eye contact, he moves his hand, gliding his fingers through my folds and unerringly finding the swollen bundle of nerves that weeps in relief at the first press of his finger. The intensity is too much and my eyes drift closed as my body centers on the way his finger circles my clit.

"You're fucking soaked for me, aren't you?" he asks, changing the rotation of his finger until I arch my back off the couch.

"Mmmm."

"You like my fingers?" He presses one inside until it's buried knuckle deep.

White light sizzles behind my eyes. "*Yes*. Please yes." I want to beg, to weep, to get him to keep going and not stop.

A second finger joins the first and my muscles spasm around the digits.

"Mmm," he moans, pressing his lips against my hip.

With sure movements, he uses his other hand to shift me again until his shoulders rest between my thighs.

"If you like my fingers, Hayley, you're going to love this."

His tongue snakes out, tracing me from back to front, and the white light explodes in another flash, hinting at a brighter explosion just out of reach.

"God," I moan, finding his hair with my fingers, holding him in place.

He repeats the caress while pistoning his fingers and focusing on the hard bundle of nerves. First rotating his tongue around it, then tapping it in a rhythm only he can hear. When I'm writhing, he transitions to flat licks of his tongue like I'm a delicious dessert that he can't get enough of.

The moment I get used to one sensation, he changes it up, though he doesn't slow the relentless pace of his fingers. The orgasm grows brighter and hovers at the edges, teasing me with more.

"You're going to come for me," he promises, his lips brushing my sensitive flesh.

"I...Jagger. *Please.*" I want to say I know that, but all I can manage is his name as air pants in and out of my lungs in breathless gasps.

Driving his fingers deeper than before, he curls them up, finding a spot that creates a wall of light in front of my eyes. A light that should be too bright, but only drives me higher. If this is heaven, I'll gladly stay right here. On the edge with his fingers in my pussy and his tongue on my clit.

Of their own accord, my hips pulse and my body pushes, still seeking a relief that only he can provide.

He latches on to my clit and sucks, picking up the pace with his fingers.

The world around me shatters. The wall of light bursts into flames, burning me until all that's left is ashes of pleasure that rebuild, hurtling me higher. I sink my teeth into my lip to stifle the scream of pleasure that threatens to erupt as he works me through the best orgasm of my life.

I drift back slowly, like reemerging from water, piece by piece until I lie spent on the couch. I reach for him and he grabs my hand, pressing a heated kiss against my palm. When I can open my eyes, I reach for his erection, but he shakes his head.

"For you. Only for you."

Jagger Brooks has ruined me for other men. Including all the book boyfriends who used to be such good company.

What the hell am I going to do now?

# CHAPTER 9

## HAYLEY

"*A*re you sure Shep can handle Maisie?" I ask Jade as we perch on stools at The Sweetest Thing, Aspen Falls' bakery.

The bakery is adorable and smells like heaven on earth, but despite being in my comfort world of carbs, sugar, and chocolate, I can't stop worrying about how Shep will handle my precocious, curious five-year-old.

We left Maisie along with Declan and Teddy with Shep for the morning so we could run wedding errands. I'm not worried about Declan—he assumed his usual posture and was slouched over his phone with headphones on before we left. Maisie, on the other hand, was giving Shep a rundown of her favorite Paw Patrol characters and what color and vehicle were associated with each one.

God help him.

"He'll be fine. He doesn't have a ton of experience with kids, but he'll learn. I'm sure Maisie will have him whipped into shape by the time we get back." She giggles.

The image of my pint-sized tornado ordering around Jade's tall, muscular mechanic fiancé makes me laugh.

"Okay, ladies, here we go." The owner of the bakery sets a small plate of cakes with various smears of icing flavors next to each of us.

"Oh my gosh, Betty, these look amazing. What's what?" Jade leans forward to sniff the confections in front of us.

"Vanilla, chocolate, red velvet, coconut, lemon, and strawberry." She points to each one as she lists them. "I just found a recipe for this one"—she gestures to a tan iced square—"it's a spiced pear cake with chai tea icing. I've thought about turning it into a cupcake flavor, but we could do it as a wedding cake too. Sample them, then let me know what you think. I'll be in the back if you need me."

She bustles through the swinging door, and Jade and I are alone again.

"Yum." Jade picks up the first square and pops it into her mouth.

Just looking at all the decadent items has my hips expanding. Not that Jagger seemed bothered by them.

The other night was mind-blowing. From the beginning, sex with Rob was mundane—lights out, in bed, a handful of positions —and that was before we had Declan. He never once had me sprawled out and naked on the couch the way Jagger did while he worked magic on—and in—my body with his tongue. And my ex never would have pleasured me without expecting it in return.

Things haven't gone further—or even as far—as that night since, but we have had two amazing make-out sessions on my front porch. Both had me clenching my thighs as desire thrummed through my body. Even now, I'm haunted by the feeling.

Jagger is so different from what I was used to. It's like he can't get enough—like I'm better than any of the samples laid out in front of me.

"Oh my God, Hayls, have you—" Jade opens her eyes and zeroes in on me. "What's wrong?"

"Wrong?" I ask, caught off guard by her question.

She waves a hand over my plate. "You haven't tasted anything yet."

Heat fills my cheeks. I've been so caught up in reliving my kisses with Jagger, I got distracted.

"Sorry." I pop the first sample into my mouth, and the flavors of cinnamon, pear, and the ginger and clove from the chai burst on my tongue.

Jade goes from concerned to curious as she stares at me.

I finish chewing the bite under her intense scrutiny and swallow. "What?"

"Ordinarily you wouldn't need a second invitation to dive into German chocolate." She points at the cake with the coconut smear next to it.

She's right. But I try to play off my choice as more thoughtful than what it was.

"I wanted to try the spiced pear one. It sounded interesting. I'll save my German chocolate piece for last."

She quirks a brow. That single look has sweat beading at the base of my spine.

Shit.

"So you choose the exotic one instead? I thought you didn't like chai."

"N-no, I like—"

"Cut the crap, babe. We've been friends too long." Pursing her lips, she studies me. "Is it Rob? I swear he's the biggest asshole. If—"

"It's not Rob," I blurt, unable to contain myself.

Jade's right. She and I *have* been friends for a long time. She's my closest friend, and I've been dying to talk through this situation with her but didn't want to do it over the phone.

"It's Jagger," I whisper, peering over my shoulder to be sure I'm not heard.

She leans in so far she almost falls out of her chair. "Jagger?" Eyes wide, she straightens and tilts her head to one side.

I nod. "I—"

"He better be on his best behavior or I swear to God, I'll have Shep kick his ass."

Having witnessed how much Shep dotes on Jade, I believe he would.

I bite back a grin. "You could absolutely say he's been on his best behavior."

"Why would I say— Ew. What? Jagger?" She rears back, wrinkling her nose, her hand paused halfway to her mouth with another cake sample dangling from her fingers.

"Yeah." I snag my own piece, swirling the chocolate cake in the coconut frosting. The combination of flavors on my tongue elicits a moan from deep within me.

Jade chews through her own piece. "You know he's a playboy, right? According to Shep he's like an alpine slide. Every tourist has taken a ride."

I burst out laughing at the analogy and nearly choke on the remnants of cake. Grabbing my water, I take a gulp to clear the crumbs from where they tickle my throat.

"It's nothing serious. I figured with his swagger the story was probably something like that."

"So if it's not serious, what is it?" she asks, sitting back on her chair.

I shrug. "I—"

"You girls doin' okay?" Betty pokes her head through the kitchen door.

"Yes," we say in unison.

"Still can't believe you two are gettin' married. I remember when y'all were terrorizin' the town with your bicycle shenanigans."

"It was more than just Shep and me," Jade says, though she's smiling wide.

Betty chuckles. "Yes, I know. Even then I could tell that boy was sweet on ya."

A timer sounds behind her, and she disappears behind the door once again.

"Not sure when she'll be back so talk fast. Tell me everything." Jade pops the last sample into her mouth like a piece of popcorn.

Butterflies flutter in my belly, but I take in a deep breath to calm the sensation. "There's not much to tell."

She presses her lips together, nonplussed. "You hated him at the barbecue."

"I did not!" My voice is louder than I intend and I drop it back down to a whisper. "I did not."

"Oh really?"

"Before that night, definitely," I admit. "But then he apologized to Maisie and me—"

"He apologized to you?"

"Yeah, when I answered the door."

"Good." She nods, eyeing the kitchen door like Betty might appear any second. "Go on."

"I told you about how he brought Maisie home when she scraped her knee, right? That night, the kids and I made s'mores. After they were in bed, I was outside, keeping an eye on the fire as it died out. He came home from work and we talked."

"And?" Her entire face brightens and she perks up as she waits for my answer.

"He kissed me."

And holy shit can that man kiss—as he's proven several more times since then. I squirm as my panties dampen just remembering our last make-out session.

"So you held off on German chocolate because of a kiss? Damn, girl!"

"More than a kiss," I mumble and pop my last piece in.

"*What*? Are you telling me you had *sex* with Jagger?"

"No, well...kind of."

"Kind of? How do you *kind of* have sex with somebody?"

"The day after the kiss he showed up and took the kids and me to Misty Lake for the day. He even wanted Teddy to come too."

She presses a hand to her chest. "Aww."

I'm glad I'm not the only one who melted at the way he included the dog.

"Right? We stayed all day. He had packed enough food for lunch, snacks, dinner, you name it. Since the kids were passed out by the time we got home, he helped get them to bed—"

"And helped you to bed too?" She waggles her eyebrows.

"Jade!"

Based on the warmth in my face, my cheeks have to be fire-engine red. I check the kitchen door, which stays blissfully shut.

"Would you get to the good stuff?" She throws a wadded-up napkin at me.

I toss it back at her. "Stop interrupting then."

She mimes zipping her lips closed and throwing away the key.

"Smart-ass. But no, he didn't help me to bed. We hung out on the couch. He was so cute. You remember the way a guy in high school would stretch to put his arm around your shoulders?"

She nods.

"That's what he did and then we kissed and…stuff, but not sex. He said he wanted the experience to be about making me feel good."

Just the echo of those words sends goose bumps skittering down my spine. It's been a long time since Jade and I shared all the juicy details of our dates. But no date stories could ever measure up to the time I've spent with Jagger.

"And obviously he did. That's why you no longer require the serotonin rush that comes from chocolate."

"Nah. It's chocolate," I tell her, dragging my finger through some of the leftover smear.

"Chocolate isn't better than sex," she counters.

I pop my finger into a mouth and savor the taste. "Well, I wouldn't know, would I?"

She slaps a hand on the table. "Why not? What are you waiting for?"

"He's had to work." A sad sigh escapes me.

"So?"

"So what about the kids? What would they think if they woke up and he was there? We've kissed since that night, but that's it. Then he goes home and I go to bed."

"Hmm. Have you considered that maybe you're overthinking this? Maybe you should just let whatever happens happen. It doesn't have to be a relationship. Just a fling. Getting back on the horse and all that." She shoots me an overexaggerated wink.

Am I overthinking what's going on between us?

Declan and Maisie have already been through enough. I don't want to add to their pain by throwing Jagger into the mix, especially because this is just a temporary situation. So, yeah. A fling. Like Jade said. Why not?

*Does it have to be? Stop overthinking things, Hayley.*

Jade interrupts that train of thought. "Shep and I could have the kids over for a sleepover."

"I can't ask you to keep my kids overnight so I can get laid."

What kind of mom would that make me?

*A satisfied one.*

"You didn't ask. I offered."

"What is Shep going to think?"

"He loves me, and he'll love spending time with the kids. It'll be fine. No, it'll be fun."

Could I do this? Have sex with Jagger?

Fuck, yes.

Instantly, heat rushes through me and centers at my core. That's all I need to know. My body is one hundred percent on board with this plan.

"Have you decided?" Betty asks, stepping through the kitchen door with a large tray of chocolate-frosted cupcakes balanced in her hands.

Jade studies me for a moment before nodding.

"I have. What do you think, Hayley?"

"I think so."

It looks like I have a sleepover to plan.

# CHAPTER 10

## JAGGER

*Rose's brown eyes heat as I trace a finger along her pale pink lips.*
*"Do you know how badly I want to kiss you?" My voice is hoarse as I*
*speak around the lump of desire crushing my throat.*
*She tilts her head to the side and moves closer, lifting her hands to my*
*biceps.*
*"As badly as I want you to?" Her lips brush against my calloused finger*
*as she speaks, adding more fuel to the fire that burns through me.*
*No, through the both of us.*
*"Do you want to kiss me?" I want her to take the lead. To show me that*
*she's in this as much as I am.*
*"I—*

*I* startle in my chair at the knock on my door. "Goddammit."

The scene I just started has been firing through my blood, begging to be written. Only Rose isn't the female main character I initially started with. Gone are the blonde hair and blue eyes.

Now, Rose is Hayley. And the male main character, Sam, is me. And he was about to do all the things I've been dreaming of doing with Hayley for the last week. Since my first taste of her.

I don't want to rush her despite how fast things moved that night in her living room. Which is why I've kept the kisses we've shared to her front porch and somewhat PG.

I lock my computer and head downstairs, praying that whoever is at the door can be gotten rid of quickly. I asked Becky to cover my shift tonight and train my latest part-timer after the need to write had overridden everything else.

For the last week, when I haven't been hanging out with Hayley, I've either been at the bar or in front of my laptop, unleashing the words at a rate my fingers can barely keep up with as Rose and Sam's story takes shape. My plan tonight is to write for another hour and then see if Hayley and the kids want to grab a pizza from The Sassy Slice.

But my unexpected visitor is fucking with that plan.

Every plan to get rid of the person on the other side of the door disappears when I pull it open to find Hayley standing there. The sun shines off the lake, backlighting her in angelic pinks and peaches. Her brown hair has been smoothed into waves that drift along her shoulders and drag my attention to the V of her dress. It's what I would describe as a flirty summer dress. The thick straps on the shoulders blend into the floral pattern of the fabric. The V between her breasts hints at cleavage I damn sure would love to explore again, and the full skirt skims along her thighs.

She's sexy as fuck in an understated way. Her natural beauty ties my tongue and makes me forget everything but her.

With her, I forget to be the playboy I've trained myself to be. I just want to be with her.

"Hi," she says, smiling shyly.

That single word has me homing in on her lips and the berry color there.

Would they be sweet like berries if I dipped my head for a kiss?

"H-hi. Did we make plans and I forgot?" I glance down at the cargo shorts and T-shirt I tossed on this morning.

Uncertainty flickers on her face, and she wrings her hands. "No. Sorry, I shouldn't have—"

Grasping her hand, I yank her inside. Then I back her against the door.

"Did I tell you how much I like surprises?" I murmur, closing the distance between us until my lips tease hers.

Fuck. It's like everything I've been writing buzzes under my skin, begging to be released. She's my muse.

But this feels like more than just any ordinary hook-up.

Her chest lifts with her quick intake of breath, the hitch audible. "No."

"Well, I do." I drag my nose along her jawline, inhaling the citrusy scent that clings to her.

"Oh." She clutches my arms, and her nails prick into the sensitive skin there.

Exactly like in the scene I was just writing.

"What are you doing here?" I drop my hands to her hips and align our lower bodies.

"Ah...Shep and Jade asked to keep the kids for a sleepover and—"

That's all I need to hear. I cover her mouth with mine, and she opens for me, just as hungry for the kiss as I am. The whimper that escapes her as our tongues duel stays locked between us as I angle her head and deepen the kiss while pressing her farther into the door and eliminating the sliver of space between us.

Sleepover. The kids are spending the night somewhere else. But I don't want to make any assumptions. I break the kiss, but can't break the connection entirely, so I move my mouth to the warm skin of her neck when I finally respond.

"Does you showing up here mean what I think it does?"

"Mmm...hmm." Her fingers find my hair and hold my head in

place as I nip at the spot on her neck I've discovered is one of her more sensitive places.

She's like my personal drug. Impossible to stay away from even if I wanted to. And now she's telling me I can have an unlimited supply of her. But she's going to set the pace. My dick isn't the one in charge here.

I straighten and frame her face with my hands, leaning in while I wait for her to open her eyes.

"We can take this at your speed, gorgeous. Maybe we could start with dinner and—"

"Or maybe we could skip the pleasantries and go to bed." She moves closer, twining her arms around my neck and lifting on tiptoes to find my ear with her tongue. "And not to sleep."

Heated desire courses through me. Fuck. Her boldness is such a turn-on. I drop my hands to her ass and squeeze, pulling her closer until my erection makes itself known and pulls a gasp from her.

"What do you think?" I growl.

I hold my breath, waiting for her answer.

"Take me to bed, Jagger."

She doesn't need to tell me twice. Bending my knees, I lift her at her thighs and sling her over my shoulder.

She squeals and smacks my ass. "What are you doing? I'm in a dress!"

"That's right, you are."

I tug the dress up to her hips and band one arm around her thighs. With my free hand, I caress her smooth, warm skin until I palm the fabric of her panties.

"Jagger." She moans my name in a way that makes my dick pulse in my shorts, ready to rip through the fabric.

I rub the silk of the material and take the stairs as fast as I can. Halfway up, I slip my fingers under the hem of her panties and squeeze the warm flesh beneath.

She mewls and squirms and mimics my move, shifting her hand below the band of my shorts and boxers.

"Fuck, baby." I hustle the rest of the way up the stairs.

My vision tunnels to my door at the end of the hall.

"Turnabout is fair play," she says with a pinch to my ass.

I rush into my room, already moving her as we cross the threshold. As I ease her down the length of my body, I claim her mouth.

"You're fucking sexy as hell," I murmur, keeping her pressed tight against me. I trace her jawline with my lips before moving down her neck.

"Mmm." She tilts her head back and digs her nails into my neck to hold me in place.

Like I have any intention of letting her go now. Every other time I've kissed her, I've known the end had to come. Usually with her coming too. But tonight, I don't have to. And that fact has my body kicking into a higher gear.

I refuse to put any other name to this, but fuck, I want her with a desperation I haven't experienced before.

"Do you know how badly I've wanted this? Wanted you? How many times I've imagined you here like this?" I growl against her damp skin, already gripping the fabric of her dress and dragging it up and out of my way.

It feels amazing to say those words out loud, to not just type them as they come from the hero's mouth on the page. In some ways, all my sexual frustration has been released vicariously through him. But not tonight.

Tonight is all about her and me. About all the ways I can make her breathe my name in ecstasy.

She shivers as the cool air brushes her exposed thighs.

"As much as I did?" She gasps when I nip at the tendon where her shoulder and neck meet.

I've managed to work the dress up past her stomach despite

the way my hands itch to drop the fabric and cup her breasts through the lace of her bra that rubs against the back of my hand.

"More," I tell her.

With one last press of my lips to the ridge of her collarbone, I step back. I tug the dress with me until it hangs limply from my hand. She's clad in a pair of pale pink panties and matching bra, her skin flushed while her chest heaves with each breath.

My dick presses against the zipper of my shorts so fiercely I'm convinced I'll split the damn things before I can get them off.

"Fuck." I drop the dress and take her in from head to toe. Rounded hips, full breasts, lips swollen from my kisses. But it's her eyes that draw me back toward her. The molten-chocolate color calling me like a siren's song. I close the distance and cup her jaw, tilting her head up.

Every word in my brain, every line I could use disintegrates when she pins me with a look full of honest desire.

What is this woman doing to me?

"You're so fucking beautiful," I say, my voice hoarse.

A soft smile curves her lips as she tangles her fingers in my hair. Tingles course through me when she scratches her nails along my scalp. When her breasts press against my chest, I curse the fabric still in my way.

"I—" Words escape me. All I can do is capture her lips with mine, desperate to show her what I can't find the words for.

I've earned my reputation as a man-whore. But I've never craved another taste of a woman the way I do with Hayley.

Wrapping an arm around her waist, I pull her backward with me. With my free hand, I work the clasp of her bra. My fingers— normally dexterous and nimble—fumble like I'm a teenage boy doing this for the first time. Frustrated with the lack of progress, I stop beside the bed and use both hands to rid her of the offending garment.

Before I can strip it from her body, she pushes against my chest and I fall on my ass on my bed.

"Allow me," she says. The impish grin she gives me as she lifts her arms up and behind her is all the proof I need that she realized my struggle.

The bra loosens and she slips the first strap off one shoulder, followed by the other, but leaves her arms crossed in front, barely concealing her chest with the remaining fabric.

"What?" I ask.

"Lose the shirt, Jagger."

Without hesitation, I tug at the back of the neck and toss it behind her.

With that done, she drops her arms. I'm pretty sure the lacy material drops to the floor next to her. But I can't take my eyes off her breasts. The pink tips tighten under my scrutiny, making my mouth water in turn. She lifts a finger and waves it, garnering my attention.

When I'm focused on her face again, she gives me a sexy smile, then works her hands down to her hips. Once again, my focus is drawn down as she shimmies out of her panties. Then she's standing naked in front of me.

I surge up and wrap my arms around her, then I pull her back with me onto the bed, fusing my mouth to hers in hungry kisses that grow more urgent at the friction of her nipples dragging across my chest.

"You need to get naked."

She moans as I pinch one stiff peak and twist.

"Soon," I tell her. Leaning up, I capture the other breast in my mouth, tonguing her nipple before I tug at it with my teeth.

She bucks her hips and rubs her pussy against me. "Now."

I'm already reaching for the button on my shorts. The relief as my shorts loosen is almost instantaneous, but my dick isn't going to stop until I'm buried inside her. She's on her hands and knees above me, her breasts swaying seductively while I push my shorts and boxers down and kick them free.

*Don't mind if I do.*

I suck a swollen tip into my mouth, tonguing and sucking at the hard bud until her arms begin to shake and she lowers her pelvis to mine.

The heat of her pussy—so close to where I want it—is enough to break the connection. In one quick move, I roll us until she's underneath me. The image of her, tan skin from our day at the lake and brown curls fanning against my navy sheets, burns itself into my brain. Her hands roam my chest, the touch fanning the flames already burning inside me, then one slides to my ass while the other wraps around my cock. Stars flash in my vision as she squeezes and drags her hand along the length.

"Fuck, baby," I groan.

Lowering my body weight to my forearms, I press kisses along her jaw until I reach the sensitive skin just below her earlobe. I roll my hips so my dick glides through her folds. Fuck, the sensation is so intense I have to grit my teeth and bury my face in her neck to keep from sliding in to the hilt right now.

She tilts her head to grant me better access, and I follow her neck down with hot, open-mouthed kisses while I hold her hips steady. If she keeps up with the movements, I won't be able to maintain the control I so desperately want to hang on to.

"Please. I need you. Inside me." Her words come in pants, and her back bows off the bed.

I shift and bring my hand between her legs. "You're so wet," I tell her, finding the hard bundle of nerves.

She mewls as my thumb drags along it. "*Jagger.*"

"Soon," I promise.

I rotate my thumb around her clit, pushing against it randomly until her hips writhe against me. Without stopping, I sink one finger inside her.

Her pussy walls spasm around me in response. Putting more pressure on her clit, I add another finger. The muscles contract as I scissor them back and forth, and every muscle in her body locks. In the next instant, she screams her release, my name breaking on her lips as the orgasm barrels through her.

"That's it, baby. Come on my fingers." I don't stop until the pleasure ebbs and only then lift them to my lips and lick them clean.

"You taste so fucking good," I tell her.

Her cheeks are pink and her chest heaves as she regards me. I crawl up her body and find her mouth and she sucks at my tongue, tasting herself and me.

Would she suck my cock just as greedily?

My dick may be on board, but there's no fucking way I'm going to last with her mouth anywhere near me. I reach out blindly, finding the handle on my nightstand drawer, and grab the smooth foil packet.

"Are you ready for me, Hayley?" I ask, lifting the packet into her line of sight.

She nods. "Yes. Now. Please."

I put the corner of the foil packet between my teeth and rip it open as I lean up. Then I swiftly put it in place and settle back between her thighs.

"It's been a while since...well, except for my vibrator..." The pink that colors her cheeks is the brightest yet.

But the image of her with a toy between her legs?

"Just the thought of you with that is so goddamn hot," I tell her.

"Really?"

"Mmm." I drop a kiss to the tip of her nose. "Maybe we can try that sometime?"

"Y-you want..." Her mouth drops open in surprise.

"Baby, I want you any way I can get you. But my only focus is on your pleasure. Speaking of..." I notch my dick at her opening and press forward.

She moans and her eyes flutter shut.

"Fuck, you're so fucking tight." Gritting my teeth, I move another inch, then stop, letting her get used to my size.

Then, inch by excruciatingly slow inch, I drive forward, stretching her until my pelvis meets hers.

"Okay?" I ask.

"Mmm-hmm." Her eyes are squeezed shut, her teeth digging into her lower lip.

Sweat drips down my temples, and the muscles in my arms are locked in an effort to keep my movements slow. She jolted a few times as I pressed forward, even as she palmed my ass and pulled me closer. I need to know that she's experiencing the same pleasure I am from being inside her. Even now, her walls grip my cock like a vise. I'm keeping my own orgasm at bay by sheer will alone.

"Open your eyes, Hayley."

Her lashes flutter and lift to reveal eyes filled with pleasure, though the twinge of discomfort that accompanies it is what I'm most concerned about.

"Are you sure this is okay? I don't want to hurt you."

She nods and grasps my biceps.

"Please. I want this. You're bigger than—"

"No one else's name belongs in this bed," I tell her.

I hold still and wait for the stiffness in her muscles to relax. For the discomfort to dissipate.

Only when her eyes are filled with nothing but desire do I drop my mouth to hers and claim her lips. Then I retreat slowly and push back in. She moans, flexing her fingers against the back of my arms when my hips bump hers again.

"Let me hear you, baby." I retreat again, this time almost all the way out, before I drive back in.

"*Jagger.*"

The walls of her pussy pulse around me. She's fucking close.

"I know, baby. I can feel it. Your pussy is telling me what I need to know." Another retreat and snap forward.

94

"Oh my God," she whimpers.

"Not God, Hayley. It's only me." This time on my retreat, I drop my lips to her breast and suck the nipple into my mouth until my cheeks hollow with the suction.

With my hips thrusting forward, I sink my teeth into her flesh. That's all it takes for her to detonate around me. I grip her hips and piston mine as her orgasm continues to pulse through her and around me.

"I—I—*Jagger*." Another orgasm racks her body.

I pick up my pace, working her through this one as I let go. My orgasm rushes down my spine and into my balls.

I flex my fingers against her hips. "Fuck, Hayley."

Those are the last words I utter before the pleasure takes over, shattering in a kaleidoscope of white light and electric arcs of ecstasy that keep my hips moving even after we're both spent.

As reality creeps back in, the first thing I notice is the way Hayley rubs my back—as if that simple act alone brings her bliss. Rolling us, I dispose of the condom and toss it onto the floor to take care of later. She leans her head on my shoulder and I trace absent-minded patterns on her arm.

"Are you staying?" I ask.

She lifts her head and regards me. If I thought she was sexy before, it's nothing compared to the just-fucked glow that she sports now.

"Is that okay?"

"Okay? It's a goddamn requirement." I sit up to tug her upright next to me.

"Where are we going?" she asks as I lead her into my bathroom.

My dick is already pulsing back to life. "I'm about to clean you up so I can make you dirty again."

"Doesn't that defeat the purpose?" Her breath catches as her attention drifts to my already hardening cock.

"Not the way I do it, baby."

# CHAPTER 11

## HAYLEY

*I* wake up slowly, sensations shimmering around me along with the sunlight that filters into the room and solidifying as memories of the night before coming back to me.

Putting on that flirty dress.

The kiss Jagger laid on me when he realized what was going on.

Our first time.

My thighs squeeze together, the muscles twinging from the lack of use. It's been a long time.

*In fact, I'm pretty sure I used muscles last night that have never been worked before.*

It took time to adjust to Jagger's size. But he made sure to go slow and build the pleasure until it surrounded me. He's an enigma. A playboy on the outside, but full of sweetness. Our shower was steamy in more ways than one, and after, we both collapsed into bed exhausted.

He woke me up in the middle of the night, already expertly playing my pussy, then slid into me from behind. The whole experience held a dreamlike quality, and damn if my core doesn't pulse at the possibility for more.

When I reach out, I expect to find Jagger, warm and sleepy next to me. Instead, I'm met with semi-cool sheets. I blink my eyes open and adjust to the light, and sure enough, there is an indent of his head in the pillow, but he's nowhere to be found.

"Good morning, beautiful."

I twist at the sound of his voice behind me, the sheet tangling around my waist, and find him standing in the doorway.

His focus dips to my breasts and the fire in his gaze reignites the desire that blazed through me last night.

"Good morning," I murmur.

The moment stretches between us and my breasts tingle under intense study.

Finally, he squeezes his eyes shut and groans.

"Fuck, Hayley, I'm about to say screw breakfast."

"And screw me instead?" I ask.

His eyes fly open as a bark of laughter escapes him. "Christ. I'm trying to be good here. I made breakfast." He lifts the tray.

My stomach chooses that moment to growl, reminding us both that we didn't eat dinner last night.

With a sigh, I yank the sheet free and tug it up to cover my chest.

"I don't know whether to be relieved or disappointed," he tells me and shuffles into the room.

I smile up at him as he lowers the tray to the bed. "That makes two of us."

He leans over and presses a kiss to my lips. It's full of the promise of heat but chaste in its execution.

"Don't pout. Eat." He gestures to the tray filled with two cups of coffee, a bagel, and a bowl of fruit.

I pick up the lighter shade of coffee and try not to swoon too much.

"Creamer?" I ask.

His smile is a combination of sweet and smirk.

"I may have grabbed your flavor from the store," he admits.

"Feeling pretty cocky?" I take my first sip.

He barks out a laugh.

"Hopeful. I'd just say I was hopeful."

He settles next to me on the bed carefully to avoid jostling the tray.

"You take yours black." I gesture toward his dark brew.

"Like my soul," he jokes and lifts his own cup.

I roll my eyes. "Not what I meant. You bought this for me. What if I never had coffee over here?"

"Then I'd have brought it to your place," he says like it's a natural order of things, but it's not natural.

Not for me. I'm not used to thoughtful gestures like this.

"I don't understand you," I tell him and pick up half the bagel.

"What's to understand? I'm pretty simple."

"You'd like everyone to believe that, wouldn't you?"

He pauses in the act of popping a bite of melon into his mouth and studies me.

"Why do you say that?" The words are slow, hesitant, as if he doesn't want to know the answer, but can't help but ask it.

I set my coffee cup down on the nightstand and rest my cheek against my knees.

"You want people to think you're a playboy. Like that first day when I thought your house was mine."

I'd written him off. A shallow guy I didn't have the time or the heart to deal with.

"But then after you acted like a dick to me and to Maisie, you apologized. You bought her bear spray. Even if it wasn't exactly real bear spray, you helped her feel better."

"It was my fault she was scared," he says.

"That's exactly what I mean. Thinking that way, going out of your way to make her feel better, proves to me that you're more than what you want people to think. There's more to you than your small-town Casanova routine."

He shrugs and pops another bit of the fruit into his mouth.

"Take this week too." I keep going, not sure who I'm trying to convince more—me or him.

He lifts a brow and chews the melon.

"The other night in my living room…" Heat filters through my blood, making me squirm against the mattress. "You could have been focused on getting yours. Or reciprocation—"

He frowns at me. "That night was all about you."

My heart stutters in my chest. "See? You thought about me. And you thought about me last night—"

"Being a thoughtful lover isn't a bad thing."

"No, it's not. It's actually a welcome change of pace after—"

He presses a finger to my lips, silencing me. "I told you last night, I don't want anyone else's name in bed with us."

I grasp his wrist and tug his hand free. Weaving my fingers with his, I give him a soft smile. "Then admit that you're more than what you let people see."

He focuses on our hands, flexing his fingers to hold mine more securely.

"Fine. Is that what you want to hear? That I'm not just a man-whore?"

"Why do you pretend to be?" I ask softly.

He sighs and closes his eyes, tracing the pulse point in my wrist with his thumb in an absent-minded caress.

"I wasn't always like this," he says at last. "Sure, in high school, I wasn't serious about relationships. I wasn't like Shep with Jade. Those two held the lock on high school sweethearts."

"It killed her when he broke up with her."

She was a wreck our freshman year of college, slowly building walls that I didn't think anyone would ever break down. Until Shep came back into her life last year.

He nods. "I figured. He wasn't any better. The few times I talked to him while he was gone, he sounded like half a person. I wasn't sure I ever wanted to go through that. And then I met Mandy."

My skin pricks with irrational jealousy at the sound of another woman's name on his lips. "What happened?"

"She was from Denver but had come up here to ski often. The year after she graduated from college, she thought it would be fun to work there for the winter."

"How old were you?" I ask.

He scoffs. "Old enough to fucking know better."

"To know better?"

"City girls come up here all the time. Especially to work at the resort. And they always leave. But I thought Mandy was different. That she'd want to stick around. She talked a lot about how much she loved Aspen Falls. I fell in love in a matter of weeks. Asked her to be my girlfriend. Figured that was the first step on the road to lifelong commitment."

The forced, bitter words make my stomach hurt. They also make me want to track down this bitch and throat punch her, but I stay silent and wait for the inevitable end to his story.

"When spring came and the resort shut down, I asked her to live with me. Not here. At the time I was bartending and lived in the apartment above the bar. She fucking laughed like I had said the funniest thing she'd ever heard. She was going home to Denver. To the boyfriend who was also moving back after spending his winter training at a different resort back east."

"Training?"

"He was a professional skier in line to go to the Olympics. He tore his ACL before the next Olympic trials."

Karma is a quick-fucking bitch when she wants to be.

"What happened to her?"

He shrugs. "No idea. She never came back here, that's for sure."

"Did you want her to come back?"

*Why the fuck would you ask that?*

His laugh holds zero humor. "Nah. By then I'd learned that

tourists were for short-term flings. And I had no desire to get my heart broken again."

My chest hollows out at his cynicism. "Oh."

He blinks and lets out a huff, breaking the tension hovering in the air around us into a thousand pieces of memories better left forgotten.

"Fuck, that was depressing," he says.

"Have you ever talked about it before?"

He shakes his head. "You're the only one who knows about Mandy."

"Oh." This time the feeling in my chest is more of an ache.

He shifts the tray and leans back, tugging me with him until I'm resting on top of him.

"Are you okay?" he asks, tucking a strand of hair behind my ear.

"Yeah."

"Really?"

I nod. "Just thinking."

He runs his hands down the length of my back and settles them on my ass. "I could give you something far more interesting to think about."

With every shift of him underneath me, the friction drives out my racing thoughts and fires my blood.

Am I okay with this just being a fling?

*Are you ready for anything more?*

Good point.

Leaning down, I nip at his lip and slide my tongue along his. He flexes his hands on my hips, and his dick twitches between my thighs.

"I could think of a few things we could do right now. Let's not waste it. I have to pick up the kids soon," I tell him.

"Fuck, why didn't you say something sooner?" He rolls us until I'm under him and trails kisses down my neck to my collarbone.

As his lips coast along my breast, I promise myself one thing.
I'm going to enjoy my time with Jagger while I have it.
The other promise I make to myself?
I'm not going to fall in love.
Tourists aren't permanent.

# CHAPTER 12

## JAGGER

*A* month ago, if I'd been asked what my plans were on the Monday night before my best friend's wedding—my only night off before his wedding—they definitely would have included at least a little debauchery in Denver. I would have taken Shep to a strip club or a casino in a neighboring town to celebrate his last few days as a single man.

Instead, I'm snuggled next to Hayley on the couch while Maisie lounges on the floor with Teddy and a giant bowl of popcorn. By the way the dog is inching closer to the bowl, I'm skeptical that it will make it past the intro to the movie Hayley cued up.

She must have the same thought, because a heartbeat later, she stretches forward, snags the bowl from the floor, and sets it next to us on the couch.

"Hey!" Maisie looks up, all five-year-old indignation in her scrunched-up nose and open mouth.

"Mais, we don't want Teddy to eat all that popcorn. He'll get sick," Hayley tells her daughter.

Maisie looks at the puppy, who's sitting innocently, attention averted, as if we didn't just catch him with his nose millimeters from the bowl. "He will?"

"Remember when he ate your entire plate of macaroni and cheese?"

Maisie scrunches her face in disgust. "Yuck."

"What happened when he ate her macaroni and cheese?" I whisper to Hayley.

She shivers as my breath tickles her neck. "You don't want to know. Not if you want to eat the stuff again in the near future."

I have a pretty good idea so leave that question alone.

"You're serious about never seeing this movie before?"

When I asked if she wanted to hang out with the kids tonight and she told me none of them had ever seen *Shrek*, I grabbed my DVD and headed over with pizzas from The Sassy Slice.

She cocks a brow and side-eyes me. "Declan and Maisie are a little young to have seen it. The movie's over twenty years old!"

"But you? Even when you were younger?"

"Nope." She pops the *P*, and the twinkle in her eye is all mischief. "Boys had the lock on ogres."

Her smile is as big as it can get and she snickers while I try to figure out what the hell just happened.

"Did you just…did you just burn me?" I ask her, not quite sure how to handle it.

"Mmm-hmm." She leans over and brushes her lips along my cheek.

If we were alone, I'd turn my head and capture those lips for myself.

We've been super cautious with the amount of affection we show each other in front of Declan and Maisie. Not that we've all been together much since our sleepover the other night. But after sitting beside her at dinner earlier and now waiting on the movie to start, it's getting hard to keep my hands and my lips to myself.

"You know I'm going to make you pay for that later, right?" I growl into her ear and nip the lobe.

"I'm counting on it." Her gaze meets mine and the mischief is now pure heat.

Ready to burn the both of us.

Fuuuuck.

How long is this movie?

"Can we start the movie now?" Maisie asks.

"We're waiting on Declan," Hayley reminds her.

"But he's been upstairs forever."

Fifteen minutes probably does feel like forever to a five-year-old who's ready to do something.

"I'll go check on him." Hayley scoots away.

With a hand on her arm, I pull her back. "You hang out here. I'll go check."

"You're sure?" She searches my face, her expression full of surprise and hope.

Was her ex that much of an asshole that he didn't ever offer to do something so simple?

Obviously the guy was an idiot for letting her go. So a discovery like this shouldn't surprise me.

I squeeze her thigh and brush a kiss to her cheek. "I'll be right back."

It's silent upstairs. The bathroom door is open, and the room is empty, so I head to his room and knock on the half-open door.

"Declan?"

The door swings open wider, and I find him standing in front of the mirror above the dresser, a tie knotted around his neck. His eyes meet mine in the mirror, but he doesn't turn.

"Just checking on if you're ready to watch the movie."

"I can't tie this." His shoulders slump. "Mom says I need to wear a tie for the rehearsal dinner but I don't know how. I watched a YouTube video and wanted to practice." His voice quivers and tears line his lashes, but they don't fall.

Without a word, I enter the room and close the door behind me.

"I tried calling my dad, but he didn't answer," he adds in a whisper.

Yep.

Grade-A Asshole.

"I could show you if you want," I offer as casually as I can.

"Really?"

I nod. "I don't wear ties often, but I've tied one or two in my day."

And had to learn from Shep's uncle since my own dad walked away from our family after Brittany was born.

I close the distance and stand next to him in front of the mirror. "May I?" I ask and motion to the tie.

"Okay." He wipes his hand along his nose and takes a deep breath. Then he lifts his head so I can access the mass of knots at his neck.

I make quick work of them, unraveling the tie and tugging it free.

"Let me just remind myself," I murmur, fumbling my way through tying it around my own neck a few times until my fingers remember the steps.

He watches quietly for several moments before shifting his attention to the mirror in front of us. "You like my mom, huh?"

My stomach drops, making me miss the correct end, and I snarl the tie. "What?"

"My mom—you like her." It's more a statement than a question.

"What makes you say that?" I ask, unsnarling the tie and finishing the knot. For a moment, I examine my handiwork, then I gesture for him to stand in front of me.

"You've been hanging around a lot."

I make a noncommittal noise in the back of my throat. "Yeah."

"And you kissed her. In the kitchen after pizza, I saw you." He keeps his attention focused on my reflection. His expression is calm, and there's no judgment in his voice.

Shit. I snuck a kiss in the kitchen when the kids were occupied—or appeared to be. So much for being careful.

"Yeah. Here, your turn."

I have him stand in front of me.

"Put your hands on mine while I go through the steps, then I'll have you try it a few times," I tell him.

"'Kay."

We work through the motions and end up with a lopsided tie, but it's a significant improvement over the knots I walked in on earlier. The concentration on his face—the way he sticks his tongue out in the corner when we get to the threading part—is all Hayley. I can't help but smile at the kid.

"Is it okay that I like your mom?" I ask.

He finishes undoing the tie and we start the process over again. "Yeah."

"I like you and your sister too. You guys are pretty cool kids."

This time when we finish, the tie is noticeably better. I step back and gesture for him to repeat the process alone.

"And Teddy?"

"Yeah, even Teddy." The smile on my face gets broader.

Declan's smile stretches his cheeks to match.

This is the first time I've seen him genuinely smile. I'm used to the teenage smirk he's perfected.

We're silent as he works through the process and finishes the tie on his own.

"I did it!" He turns to me, his eyes bright, and fuck, if I don't give a small piece of my heart to him.

"Good job, bud." I hold out a fist and he bumps it proudly.

"One more time?" he asks.

I nod. "As many as you want."

He runs through it again, faster this time. His little chest puffs with confidence and his eyes shine. "Awesome," he whispers.

I fight the smile that hovers on my lips. "You learned that a lot faster than Shep and I did when his uncle taught us," I tell him.

Warmth fills my chest. Contentment and pride in Declan consume me from the inside out.

"His uncle? What about your dad?" he asks.

I lift a shoulder and let it drop. "My dad left when I was younger. So Shep's Uncle Joe taught us all the guy stuff."

"Like what?"

I doubt Hayley wants me to tell Declan about the sex talk that Uncle Joe had with us.

"Er, you know, how to tie a tie. Stuff like that."

"Oh." He takes my answer at face value and goes back to fidgeting with his tie.

Whew. I breathe a sigh of relief. "You ready to go watch the movie now?" I ask him.

He undoes the tie and tucks it back into a drawer.

"You're sure I'm gonna like it?"

"Dude, I wouldn't have recommended it if I wasn't. Trust me?"

He nods and brushes a strand of hair out of his face. "'Kay."

We're almost to the door when I speak again.

"I was thinking about going to get a haircut tomorrow so it looks good for the wedding. I was going to ask Shep to come. You want to hang out with us?"

He turns toward me, blinking in surprise.

The ex gets upgraded to Grade-A Douchebag Asshole.

"You mean it?"

"Wouldn't have offered if I didn't," I tell him.

"I—yeah. I have to ask my mom though."

"I'll talk to her." I hold a hand out toward the door. "Let's go watch the movie. And in the morning, I'm making *waffles*."

He rolls his eyes at my bad impression of Eddie Murphy.

"Okay, Donkey."

I stop just outside his doorway.

"I thought your mom said you'd never seen the movie."

"I watched it with my friends once. It was okay."

"Okay? Only okay? How can you say that? It's one of my favorite movies."

He snorts. "Aren't you a little old to watch cartoons?"

"You're never too old to watch cartoons," I tell him.

"Are you sure?" he asks, eyes trained on me.

"Absolutely, bud," I tell him and meet his gaze for a moment before letting a smile stretch across my face. "Did you know ogres are like onions?"

I'm shooting for Mike Myers's distinctive voice with my question.

He groans, but he can't hold back the laughter that quickly follows. "That was bad."

"You have no idea."

"Finally!" Maisie says when we reach the living room.

Without a word, Declan hops into the chair, sitting in a way that has my neck aching even now.

Hayley starts the movie and leans back into my arm when I settle next to her on the couch. "Everything okay?"

"Yeah."

"Has anyone told you how special you are?" She stretches up to brush her lips against my jaw.

"How about you tell me after the kids are asleep tonight?" I waggle my brows at her.

She laughs.

"Shhh." Maisie turns around and levels us with a look of indignation.

I hold up my hand and Hayley follows suit.

When the little girl turns back to the screen, Hayley moves her mouth close to my ear.

"It's a date."

# CHAPTER 13

## HAYLEY

*E*xpedition Brewing is all earth tones and warm wood polished to a gleaming shine. Colorful taps are situated every so often along the circular bar and the glassware and bottles of liquor reflect the light hanging from above. The details that stand out the most are the hammered copper drum in the ceiling over the main dining area and the matching border along the top of the bar.

The place is just as charming as the rest of the mountain town. The scenery and slower pace everywhere I go are a welcome change from what I'm used to in the city.

"You like?" Jagger murmurs, his heat soaking into my back, and presses a kiss to my neck.

"This is really nice." I turn around and loop my arms around his neck.

Behind him, Jade appears, her brows lifted, but I ignore the look and focus back on the man in front of me.

"A labor of love."

My tummy flutters at the way his lips wrap around the word *love*.

"It was pretty bad before," Jade adds, moving close to the two of us.

"But it was the only bar in town so we all just dealt with it," Shep says from beside her.

"What was it like before?"

"Dark, sticky, and a bit…" Jade hums as if she's searching for a word to finish her description.

"Rough?" Jagger offers.

"Skeezy," she corrects. "I never came here by myself before Jagger bought it."

"And you won't have to go anywhere by yourself again," Shep tells her, pulling her into his arms.

"Hey, hey, hey, I still have one more night of freedom," she teases him, but softens her verbal jab with a kiss to his cheek.

I love the interaction between the two of them. The Jade I met in college was heartbroken over Shep. Even after she moved on, she was only part of her true self. But the large smile that stretches her cheeks now and the way her body naturally turns to her fiancé's proves just how full of life she is these days.

"Why did you buy it?"

I turn back to face Jagger, and he kisses my forehead.

*I'm not swooning, you are.*

"It seemed like a good idea. I liked bartending here."

"Because that's what you do when you like your job, you buy the place," Shep says with a roll of his eyes.

"We don't all have an Uncle Joe to gift us our own repair shop."

"You mean Uncle Joe didn't gift this place to you?" Shep teases.

"Fuck no. I bought this place with my own money."

"How the hell did you get the money to buy this place anyway? And the repairs? You become an escort and not tell anyone?"

This kind of banter between the guys, I've learned, is the

status quo, but that doesn't stop me from stiffening at Shep's suggestion.

"Asshole," Jagger growls, kneading at the new tension in my shoulder.

Even Jade shoots him a look.

"What?"

"You're an idiot," she tells him.

"What did I say?"

"I paid for the bar with my savings. And before you make any more guesses about my profession, I paid for the renovations too."

Shep's responding frown is full of confusion. "You earned that much as a bartender?"

"Dude."

Jade sighs. "Shep."

"I've always been curious." He shrugs.

Jagger arches a brow. "And you're choosing right now to ask me about it?"

"I don't know. I guess I didn't think about it too much since you did the renovations and stuff before I moved home."

Given how perfect Shep and Jade are for each other, it's hard to remember that he only moved back last year after being gone for over a decade. The breath that Jagger sucks in behind me is audible and brings me back to the present. His exhale brushes the hairs at the nape of my neck, sending a shiver coursing down my spine.

"You could have asked before now."

"Why is it some big secret? Did you break the law?"

"Shep!" Jade smacks her fiancé's arm.

"You really want to know?"

Shep roughs a hand through his hair, like maybe he's caught on to the tension his questions have created. "It's not really my business."

"But you'll probably ask again. Or continue to assume I sold my body for the money."

"Not your body." He shakes his head and scowls at Jagger. "Escorts just charge for their company, I thought."

"Jesus Christ," Jagger sighs, slumping behind me.

"Shepard," Jade groans.

"Fine. I'll tell you," Jagger says, suddenly straightening again. He clears his throat. "Consider this your wedding present. I wrote a book. Several actually."

Shep barks out a laugh but when no one else joins in, he sobers. "Seriously?" he asks.

"Yeah. Seriously."

Shep lifts an eyebrow as he studies his best friend. "Huh."

"Huh what?"

"I could see that."

"Really?" This time it's Jagger who sounds surprised.

"Yeah. You always liked English classes. You and Jade were both in the smart classes."

"You're smart, babe," Jade tells him.

"You guys did those classes. Not me. And the writing thing, that paid for all this?" Shep gestures around the dining room.

"Some. I did have some savings. And Uncle Joe may have left you the shop, but right before he died he came to see me. Gave me an envelope and told me I would know when to open it. He invested in Expedition Brewing. 'From one business owner to the other.'"

"What—"

A server steps up to us. "Are we ready to eat?"

"I'm starving," Jagger says.

"Mommy, is it time to eat?" Maisie comes up to me, the ribbon that I tied in her hair now dangling from her fingers.

"Let's go." Shep motions to the others around us, and we all take seats at the tables that Jagger had the staff push together.

He and Jade turn and find their seats, and we follow with

Maisie tugging us both forward, her little hands gripping one of each of ours. Declan is already sitting, his brown eyes visible now that his shaggy hair has been cut and styled.

"Oh no, Maisie, I'm stuck." Jagger stops abruptly and bends forward in an exaggerated way as Maisie continues to tug.

She drops my hand to double her efforts, grunting as she does.

He lifts one foot and finally lets her pull him free. "Thanks," he tells her.

Her responding giggle is infectious. She holds tight to one hand and dangles from it in excitement.

I meet the gaze of the man who inspired her happiness. The corner of his lips curve and his eyes soften. There's so much written there—happiness, indulgence...love? I suck in a breath and the word rolls around more.

Love.

Holy shit.

I'm falling in love.

With the man I wrote off as a playboy when I got here a few weeks ago.

How is that possible?

What the hell am I going to do?

"Are you okay?" The man in question shuffles closer and cups my elbow.

"What?"

"You look...panicked for lack of a better word."

Maybe that's because I am.

I didn't plan on falling for him.

But somewhere between the heated kisses and his sweet, genuine interactions with my kids, I did. Or at least I'm starting to.

"Hayls?"

That's it. I'm a goner. It's a nickname that very few people use. My family. Jade.

People who are close to my heart.

"I'm sorry, I'll be right back. Bathroom?" I ask him, though I can't quite meet his eye.

"Back there. Are you sure you're okay?" He frowns, brows pulled low, and moves close enough that his spiced bergamot smell wraps around me.

"I'm fine." Though the high-pitched tone of my voice says otherwise. I clear my throat. "I'm fine." There. Better. "I'll be right back."

Before he can ask again, I turn and scurry away. Once I'm safely inside the bathroom, I stare at myself in the well-lit mirror.

"What are you doing?" I ask my reflection.

"That's what I was coming in here to find out," Jade says, pushing through the door.

My heart lurches into my throat. "What are you doing in here? You should be out there. It's your rehearsal dinner," I tell her.

"Yeah?" She crosses her arms over her chest. "Well, when my maid of honor ran toward the back of the restaurant like her feet are on fire, I figured I should find out why. What's going on?"

"I..." The way my heart pounds against my chest makes it a challenge to breathe, let alone talk.

"You?" she asks, leaning back against the wall.

I pull in a deep breath and let it out slowly. "I'm falling for him," I whisper and cover my face, still trying to come to grips with all of it.

"Jagger?" she whisper-shouts. "You're falling for Jagger?"

"Uh-huh." I drop my hands and force myself to face my best friend.

Her face brightens, and with a squeal, she launches herself at me in a hug. "That's so exciting!"

"Exciting? How is it exciting? This was supposed to be a fling. I live in the Springs," I remind her.

"But you said yourself that you love the town and you like the pace. You can tutor from anywhere. I'm sure you can finish your degree online and—"

"I do like the town, but I don't know how he feels." I swallow past the lump in my throat. "Maybe he wants to keep this casual." Jagger has always been a casual guy. Why would that change now?

"I don't think so. I saw the way he was with you and Maisie and Declan. I think he's falling for you too."

I huff a breath, my mind reeling. "I can't just pick up and move the kids."

"Why not?" she asks.

"I…"

Only no real reason comes to mind.

Instead, I picture them at Misty Lake. Maisie throwing a stick for Teddy, and Declan fishing off the dock. The two of them lounging on the floor in the living room while Jagger and I cuddle on the couch during family movie nights.

Why can't that be my future? Our future?

"Hayley?"

I blink and the vision disappears.

"Huh?"

"You need to talk to Jagger."

"What if he doesn't feel the same?"

"But what if he does?"

⚏ ⚏ ⚏

"You're quiet," Jagger murmurs as we're driving home after the rehearsal dinner.

Jagger offered to drive my car tonight, so I've been staring out the window at the darkening landscape as it fades to black.

"Sorry. I guess I just have a lot on my mind." I turn to check on the kids. Declan is curled over his phone, and Maisie's blinking slowly as she watches out the window.

"You know there's nothing to what Shep said earlier, right?"

"Huh?" I turn to him, frowning.

The lights from the dash display his serious expression. "The comment about what I did to pay for the bar."

"Oh." I had forgotten that conversation in light of the other revelation of the night.

"I didn't." He shifts his attention to me momentarily before looking back toward the road.

"I know."

"You do?"

"Mm-hmm. I don't picture you doing that for money."

We're speaking in code given the little ears close by.

He rests a hand on my thigh and squeezes gently.

"No. I wouldn't."

Silence drops between us again, so quiet that the game Declan is playing on his phone is audible despite his headphones. Jagger turns on to the road that leads to our houses and parks the car in front of the one I've called home for the last several weeks.

"It's hard to believe we go home Monday," I say.

A small part of me hopes that he'll ask me to stay longer. That he'll want to explore what's been happening between us. Instead he turns off the ignition, but he makes no move to exit the car. And he doesn't release his hold on me. We sit side by side, neither ready to climb out, to break the connection between us.

"Uh, are we going inside?" Declan asks from the backseat.

"Yeah. Let's go, buddy." I peek back at Maisie again. She's asleep in her booster seat now, with her head slumped to one side. "Awww."

Jagger turns around as well, and one corner of his lips lifts in that smile that sets the butterflies loose in my stomach again. "I'll grab her for you."

"Thank you."

Cool air rushes along my thigh when he lifts his hand. I take a deep breath and let it out, forcing away all thoughts but those that have to do with getting inside and getting the kids to bed.

Declan steps out of the car and I join him.

"I'm going to my room to play games," he tells me.

"Will you let Teddy out before you go up?" I ask.

"Sure, Mom."

"And then not too late, okay, buddy?"

"Nope." He lopes toward the house, even more gangly than when we arrived three weeks ago. As if he's grown in such a short time.

He'll need new pants for school at this rate.

"You ready?" Jagger, who's got Maisie snuggled in his arms, her head buried under the crook of his neck, joins me.

"Y-yeah."

I lead the way, and like the night at the lake, we get her tucked in. Teddy folds himself at the foot of her bed as I pull the sheet up to her shoulders.

"Goodnight, sweet pea." I brush a kiss on her forehead.

Her little nose scrunches in her sleep but smooths out quickly.

We back out of the room quietly, and I close the door behind us.

When we're alone in the hallway, Jagger whispers, "I guess I should probably get home."

I move closer, loop my arms around his neck, and press my breasts against his chest.

"You could stay."

He pulls in a long breath, searching my eyes in the semi-darkness. "Are you sure?"

Lifting up, I brush a chaste kiss against his lips. I'm here for three more nights, and I don't want to waste them without him.

"Please stay."

# CHAPTER 14

## HAYLEY

*T*he way his eyes darken is clear despite the lack of light around us, and the charge that instantly ignites in the air is enough to burn us both to the ground.

Without releasing him, I step back quietly, moving closer to my door. When I bump into it, he lifts an arm and holds it against the solid wood. He soundlessly finds the handle with his free hand and pushes the door open. He surrounds me and I keep my arms looped around his neck. The touching is minimal, it could even be platonic. But the way his gaze stays locked with mine is anything but.

Once we've shuffled our way inside, Jagger closes the door and leans against it. With a hum, he grasps my hips and yanks our lower halves into alignment.

Electricity arcs from his body to mine, and my core pulses to life, begging for his touch. He takes advantage, dropping his head and claiming my mouth, pushing his tongue past my open lips. He flexes his hands on my hips once before following the curve of them to my ass and squeezing the flesh there through my dress and panties.

"Aren't you going to ask me?" he murmurs, trailing his lips along my jaw.

I cling to his shoulders and tilt my head to give him better access.

"Ask you what?"

Blindly, I slip my hands down his chest and work at the buttons of his shirt. With each one, I can't help but run my hands along the warm skin exposed before moving on to the next.

"What I write." He drops his mouth to my neck and nips at the skin, then laves at the bite with his tongue.

I jolt at the zap that shoots through me, and inadvertently yank a button free of the thread. It hits the floor at our feet with a ping.

"Shit."

"Don't worry about it. I have more shirts."

As if to prove his point, he grasps both sides of the shirt and yanks, sending several more buttons pinging around us. He shrugs out of the ruined cotton and drops it at our feet. My eyes and fingers vie for equal claim over the toned expanse of skin highlighted in the moonlight that filters through the windows.

He twirls me in his arms until my back is pressed to his front and his erection pushes insistently against my ass.

"Ask me," he whispers against my skin, his lips tracing along the open back of the dress between my shoulder blades.

I'm so focused on the rising lust that burns through my body, it takes several breaths for his words to make sense.

"You don't want to keep it a secret?" I ask.

"Ask me." His fingers stop with his demand, his lips finding the sensitive skin behind my earlobe.

"Jagger." I wiggle my hips against him.

"Fuck." He drops his hand to my hip, holding me hostage.

He grasps the zipper at my back and tugs it down halfway at an agonizingly slow pace while his mouth continues to tease the skin of my shoulders and neck.

"*Please.*"

"Ask. Me."

"W-what do you write?"

"Romance, Hayley. I write romance." There's a relief in his admission.

Questions swim in my brain, too fast to fully grasp as his fingers scatter them before they can fully form. He works the zipper the rest of the way down to push the dress off my shoulders.

Later. I'll ask him later. Right now, I just need him to soothe the fire he's created.

I arch my back, pushing myself farther into his touch. "Touch me."

He chuckles and thumbs my nipples over the material. "I am."

"More. I want more."

I need more, the line between want and need blurring with every stretched moment of sensation between us.

"How much more?" His voice is low, husky, more a vibration against my neck than anything.

I shimmy my dress the rest of the way off my hips, then reach back and palm him through his pants. "Everything."

He spins me again and slips a hand into my panties to palm my ass.

"What if I want it all?" He skates a finger down the crack of my ass and stops when his finger presses against the pucker there.

"Everything I have, it's yours."

"Not *it*, baby. You. You're mine." His finger penetrates a little and I gasp.

"*Jagger.*"

"Tell me." He drops his lips to my neck.

Desire swamps me. Every place he touches burns hot with need. "Please."

He slips the hand that's remained firmly on my ass cheek

down and swipes one finger through my folds. I whimper and twist against him as the sensation of that finger combined with the other adds fuel to the fire.

"Tell me."

"Yours," I pant, flexing my hands against his arms.

"Who?" He sinks his teeth into the tendon where my neck and shoulder meet and presses his index finger against my asshole at the same time.

"Me. I'm yours. Please."

He walks me backward until my calves bump the bed, then removes both hands from my panties to push them down my legs.

"Do you know how sexy you are?" he murmurs when he stands straight and works at the clasp of my bra.

With a flick of his wrist, the garment loosens, and he drags each strap down my arms until the lace flutters to the floor next to us.

He glides his fingers back up, following the line of my collarbone and dragging both index fingers in a heart around my breasts and along my sides. My breasts ache for his touch but I'm paralyzed, locked in the moment as he traces each curve like he's trying to memorize them all.

Maybe he is.

He angles in, and with a hand on my hip and the other on the small of my back, he lowers me to the bed. With a chaste kiss, he steps back and turns on the small lamp on the bedside table.

"I want to see you. To remember…"

He doesn't finish the sentence, but he doesn't have to. He's just as aware of the ticking clock as I am.

I hook my fingers into the waistband of his pants and tug. "Aren't you overdressed?"

A laugh rumbles in his chest, but doesn't dim the fire that burns deeply in his gaze. "Not for what I have in mind."

He hovers over me and latches on to one nipple, circling the tight bead with his tongue.

I tunnel my fingers in his hair, holding him to me. In response, he doubles down on his efforts, biting the distended tip and pulling.

"Oh my God," I moan.

He releases the nipple with a pop, then shifts his attention to my other breast while one hand slides between my legs. His thumb finds my clit as he presses one finger inside.

"*Jagger.*" I shift my legs wider as the orgasm begins to build.

"That's it, baby." He trails kisses down my stomach, then straightens from his crouch on the floor so he can anchor one of my feet to the bed followed by the other.

He trails kisses up one knee and then up the other before blowing softly against my pussy. But it's the look in his eyes when he peers up at me that makes my pussy throb in anticipation.

"Jagger?"

He groans and closes his eyes, gripping both of my knees. "I fucking love my name on your lips," he grits out.

"Jagger."

A shiver works its way down his spine when I say his name again. "Know what else I love?"

My heart flutters in my chest at his second use of the L word.

"W-what?"

"The way you sound when you come. The way you feel around my cock. The way your nails dig into my skin when you're close. The way you taste." His eyes darken further as he finishes the statement.

I prop myself up on my elbows in a way I hope is sexy and give him a flirtatious look as I drag my tongue slowly along my lips. "I like the way you taste too."

"Fuck, Hayls. I can't hold back."

"I don't want you to hold back."

It's as if my words are what he's been waiting for. He closes his eyes on a growl and drops between my thighs. Then he drags his tongue from back to front. When he circles my clit with his tongue, I fall back, unable to hold myself up any longer. My orgasm tingles at the edges, a white hot pleasure that continues to build with every swipe of his tongue.

I used to think toe-curling pleasure just existed in romance novels, but at this very moment, that's exactly what's happening.

Holy shit, I've never been so happy to be wrong.

He continues working my clit with his tongue while he nudges first one finger and then another inside.

*"Jagger."*

The orgasm flickers in my vision, ready to explode.

With a grunt, he shifts. He continues working my pussy with one hand while he presses the index finger of his other hand along the pucker of my ass.

I tense, but he doesn't relent. He holds that finger still, finding the spot inside my pussy that has the orgasm barreling down on me. Only then does he continue to push against the tight hole. The full sensation combined with the way he sucks my clit into his mouth is all it takes to hurtle me off the cliff. I fly up into the light that shatters into a million pieces, soaring among the stars as his tongue and fingers work me through a pleasure so intense I cry out and tears burn behind my eyes.

He slows his movements gradually as I float back to the earth. It isn't until I'm panting, arms flung out on the mattress on either side of me, that he stands from the bed and yanks at the button and zipper on his pants. Once he's kicked them and his boxers free, he pulls a foil packet from his wallet, tosses the leather onto the floor, and climbs back onto the bed on top of me.

"Are you okay?" he asks, claiming my mouth in a carnal kiss.

The flavors are a combination of him and me and I can't hold back the moan that vibrates from my throat.

"Mm-hmm." I refuse to break the kiss, needing so desperately to be closer to him than I already am.

I'm lost to the world, only vaguely aware of the crinkle of the foil. But when the head of his dick nudges my entrance and he pushes forward until his hips bump mine, I'm fully present and ready for him. Only then does he break the kiss on a moan.

"You feel so fucking good," he growls. His tongue rims my ear as he retreats and thrusts forward again.

"So do you," I pant.

I release his shoulders and slide my hands down his back to push his ass against me. "More."

He rolls us until I'm on top, gripping my hips as he pistons up into me. Another orgasm builds and with this different position, he drives into me deeper, his pelvis rubbing against my clit in a delicious slide of friction.

"Oh God." I sink my teeth into my bottom lip to dampen my moans to whimpers as he increases his speed.

He brushes his fingers against my lips, and I release the bite on a gasp. Then he finds my nape and tugs me down, claiming my lips and soothing the flesh where my teeth just were.

I fasten my mouth more fully to his as he continues to drive up into mine. We stay locked in our kiss, our tongues tangling, until my lungs demand oxygen. Sitting up, I drag air into my deprived body and balance myself on his chest.

"Fuck, I'm close." The muscles stand in relief on his neck and another tics in his jaw, as if it's taking all his control to hold back his orgasm.

"Then come," I tell him.

"No, together." He pants the words.

He grasps my hands and laces our fingers with a squeeze. Then he tugs me so that I'm leaning over him. Moving my hands to his chest, he lifts up and finds one of my breasts with his mouth while his fingers twist and tug at the other nipple.

Lightning arcs from my nipples to my core, and the muscles in my pussy tighten.

"Fuck." He pulls my nipple back into his mouth, his cheeks hollowing out with the suction. His other hand coasts down my back to my ass and kneads the flesh as he thrusts up.

Again, he slips those fingers along my crack. Slowly, he pushes at the pucker of my ass. The pressure there combined with the hard bite at my breast is all it takes. I go from building to an orgasm to falling headfirst into wave after wave of pleasure.

"*Jagger.*"

My walls grip him, my entire body locking as the orgasm crests up and over, dragging me under and pushing me free with every thrust of his hips. He grips my hips again and increases his tempo, holding me still as he thrusts one final time and growls his own release.

I fall against his chest, his heartbeat thundering under my cheek as he rubs circles along my back.

"I don't think I can move," I tell him, nuzzling his chest and pressing my lips against his calming heartbeat.

He uses his thumb and forefinger under my chin to lift my gaze to his. "So stay."

The words are there in his expression. He's not talking about right now. He's not talking about me on his chest.

"Stay?" I repeat.

Warmth travels my body. A sense of belonging and a desire to do exactly what he's asking me to do. What I want to do.

He nods and lets out a slow breath. "Don't go. I'm...falling for you, Hayley." His throat works as he regards me with nothing but affection and desire and fear in his eyes. "I realize it probably doesn't mean much coming from a man-whore like me—"

"I was thinking more that it's a really good line for a romance author," I tell him, only slightly teasing.

"I'm not going to lie, I have probably written something like that at one point in time. But I've always thought it was just an idea in a story. But you make me believe that there's more. I can't explain it, and that's hard for me to admit because I usually *do* have the words."

I fuse my lips to his to stop the stem of words.

We shift until I'm curled on his chest and his heart beats under my palm. I break the kiss slowly, reluctant to let him go.

"I'm falling for you too," I admit.

His eyes light up and we share a smile.

"So what do we do now?" he asks after several moments.

"We figure this out. You know I'm a package deal though. Me, Declan, Maisie—it wouldn't just be the two of us."

"You forgot Teddy," he says with a smile.

"Does that mean that the package deal doesn't scare you off?"

He shakes his head. "Your kids are amazing. The dog too. I want to give this a shot."

I fold my arms along his chest and rest my head on my hands.

"Then let's figure this out."

# CHAPTER 15

## JAGGER

*T*he sunlight that streams through the windows is different.

"What the fuck?" I mumble into the pillow.

I bought room-darkening curtains for a reason. It only works if I pull them shut at night. Cracking my eyes open with a little hiss, I catch sight of the pale green of the sheets. That's when it hits me. I'm not at my house.

I never went home last night. Hayley fell asleep first, her even breathing washing over my chest, and I kept telling myself to move her, to get up and go home so I wouldn't fall asleep. But between one breath and the next, I was asleep with her in my arms.

She's falling for me.

I'm falling for her.

*Fuck, admit it.*

Alright, fine. I've already fallen for her.

Her and Declan and Maisie. And even the Tasmanian devil dog they constantly call a "baby."

"Hayls?" I lift my head and check the room since she's not in my line of sight, but I'm alone.

I throw the covers back and grab my pants and boxers off the floor. My shirt comes next. I shrug into it and fasten the few buttons I didn't destroy last night.

The rest of the house is silent as I make my way downstairs. Hayley is sitting in front of her laptop at the kitchen table, knees drawn up in front of her, a mug of coffee balanced on top of them, as she reads the screen.

"Good morning, baby," I murmur, ducking low to wrap my arms around her.

She squeals and almost loses her coffee. I steady the mug and brush a kiss on her cheek.

"You startled me," she says, closing the laptop.

"I didn't mean to." I tug her up and into my arms for a hug. "I woke up and you were gone."

"Mmm. Good morning." She pops up onto tiptoes and plants a sweet kiss against my lips. "I couldn't sleep, so I came down for coffee and to do a few things."

"Stuff for school?"

She mentioned wanting to finish school now that Maisie will be in kindergarten. Her hope is to finish a degree in elementary education so she and the kids can have similar schedules.

"No. Although I need to check that the classes are starting the way the academic advisor said they would. But I was working on my blog. I haven't posted in a while and I wanted everyone to know I was too busy living my own real-life romance."

I'm too busy processing what she just said to pay much attention to the soft-eyed look she gives me.

"Blog?" The word gets stuck in my throat and sours in my mouth

"Mm-hmm." She rounds the counter with her coffee mug with no idea that tension has knotted between my shoulder blades.

"Did you want coffee?" she asks, turning toward me.

In a heartbeat, everything fades away. With the sun filtering through the window behind her, she looks angelic.

No, she looks delectable.

*Good enough to eat.*

Good thing I'm in the kitchen.

I close the distance between us. Her eyes widen as I lift her onto the counter, and her legs open, creating space for me to step between them.

"Is that a no to coffee?" she teases.

The breathy quality to her voice takes something away from the barb.

"Not yet." I plant my hands on the counter, caging her in, and capture her lips with mine.

She tastes like coffee and a flavor that's all Hayley. It's sweeter than my favorite dessert and more addictive than anything I've ever experienced. She moans and wraps her legs around my waist, tilting her head and deepening the kiss.

"Mommy, is it time to get ready yet?"

Maisie's voice reaches us a millisecond before the little girl bounces into the kitchen.

I shift back, letting Hayley's legs drop softly against the cabinet. But I leave my hands on her thighs rather than stepping away completely.

If Maisie thinks anything about it, she doesn't comment. Hair mussed and sleep lines still creasing her face, she wanders to the cupboard to grab a colorful box of cereal. Teddy bounds up to Hayley and me and shoves his nose between the two of us.

"Good morning to you too, dog," I tell him with a pat on the head.

"He probably needs to go out." Hayley slides off the counter. The move forces her to line up next to me from chest to thigh.

"I-I'll do it," I tell her.

I need a few minutes to get my dick under control.

135

◮ ◮ ◮

Hours later, I stood next to my best friend and watched him marry his soulmate. But my ability to focus on the ceremony was hindered by the beautiful woman standing just behind the bride. Our gazes locked more than once, and for the first time in a long time, the concept of doing this for myself one day didn't scare the shit out of me.

Hayley weaves between tables, headed my way, looking incredible in her pale pink knee-length bridesmaid dress.

I angle to one side as she comes closer. "Have I told you how gorgeous you look today?"

"Yes, when you came back from getting ready."

After breakfast, I went back to my place to get dressed while she got herself and the kids ready. When I stepped back into her house and found her standing in the kitchen, I couldn't find the words for how beautiful she looked.

"You don't look so bad yourself." She raises a brow and gives me a once-over.

Thankfully, Shep chose light tan suits with pale pink ties for his groomsmen rather than stuffy tuxes. I'm not a fan of the tie, so the moment bridal party photos were over, I loosened the knot. Declan is still sitting at the table, his own tie long gone. He was so proud to show me that he had tied it himself when he came downstairs this morning.

"Jade looks like a princess," Maisie says from between us, twirling in her own miniature version of a ball gown.

Shep and Jade are at the edge of the dance floor talking to Shep's mom. They just finished their first dance as man and wife, and next up is the traditional dance with the parents.

Shep promised there would be cake at some point. Once the kids get a piece, my hope is that they'll be ready to head home. Then after they're tucked in for the night, I have every intention of exploring the silky texture of Hayley's legs to find out if they're as smooth as they look under that dress.

"She sure does," Hayley tells her daughter.

"Can I have a dress like that?"

"What do you need it for?" Hayley asks.

The little girl shrugs. "I dunno. But it's pretty."

"It is." Hayley gives her daughter a warm smile, then her attention drifts to me.

My heart thumps in my chest as the vision of her in a dress like that shimmers in my imagination.

"How about I get you a dress like that when you have a reason to wear one."

"I guess."

Dropping to my haunches in front of the little girl, I tug at the fabric of her dress. "You already look like a princess in this dress."

Dark eyes that mirror her mother's light up. "Really?" She twists and turns to send the skirt rustling.

The DJ makes an announcement, and behind Maisie, other couples join Jade and her dad on the dance floor.

Looking back at the little girl in front of me, I hold out a hand.

"Really. Which is why I would be honored if you would dance with me right now, princess."

She glances up at Hayley, her smile wide and her eyes sparkling. "Can I, Mom?"

Tears rim Hayley's lower lashes, and a soft smile tilts the corners of her kissable lips. With her fingers pressed to her trembling lips, she nods. The movement causes a single tear to slip free.

Maisie grasps my hand, and I rise from my position, using a thumb to wipe the errant moisture from Hayley's cheek.

"We'll be right back." I tip in close and brush a kiss against her cheek. With that, I lead Maisie to the dance floor.

The weight of Hayley's gaze between my shoulder blades follows me the whole way there. I catch her eye again as I turn back and pull Maisie in. The words of Alan Jackson's "Always Be My Baby" float in the air around us, causing my chest to constrict.

This is what's been missing in my life. A woman who takes my breath away. And the bonuses she brings along with her. Declan and the pride that filled his eyes the other night when he tied his tie, and Maisie, who's got her chin tucked as she looks down at her feet and mine.

"You doing okay, Maisie?"

She tilts her head back, and concentration knots between her brows. "It's hard."

I bite my lip to keep from smiling at the way those two words grit between her teeth.

"How about I help?"

With her lips pressed together, she gives me a succinct nod. "'Kay."

I stop in the middle of the floor and step closer. "Stand on top of my feet."

"Won't that hurt? Declan says it hurts when I step on his foot."

I can't help but smile at her. "I'll be okay. Just try it."

She puts her left foot on top of my right one tentatively, and her little fingers grip my hands as she brings the right one up and settles it on my left.

"Hold on tight," I say.

And then I rotate us around the dance floor. Her smile comes back full force. During one particularly wild turn, we bump into Shep, who's standing at the edge of the dance floor watching Jade and her dad finish their dance. Maisie tosses her head back and laughs when he lets out an exaggerated *umph*.

Once we've spun away again, he calls out, "Looking good, Brooks."

"Don't we know it," I fire back, and Maisie's giggle fills the air around us again.

As the music fades, I stop and lift her into a hug.

"Thanks for the dance, princess."

She tightens her arms around my neck. "That was so much fun!"

I lower her to her feet at the edge of the dance floor, and once she's free of my hold, she races to her mom and throws her arms around Hayley's waist.

Hayley hugs her daughter back, but a heartbeat later, Maisie pulls away and rushes toward Declan.

"Seems like she had fun," I say, closing the distance between us.

This time it's Hayley who throws her arms around my neck.

"That was the sweetest thing I've ever seen." She pulls my lips down to hers for a kiss that we lose ourselves in.

As our tongues tangle in their own type of dance, I want nothing more than to find a quiet corner so we don't have to stop. But there'll be time for that later when it's just the two of us. With Herculean effort, I shift the intensity of the kiss from passionate to chaste before pulling away completely.

Her lashes flutter along her cheekbones before they lift. Everything I'm feeling—desire, love, contentment—they're all reflected in the warm brown that I want to drown in.

Earlier we talked about figuring this out with her in the Springs and me here. But how the fuck am I supposed to let her go when all I want is to ask her to stay?

# CHAPTER 16

## HAYLEY

"*M*ommy?" Maisie's eyes are on the downward droop, but she's putting up a valiant effort against the pull of sleep.

"Yes, baby?"

"Do we have to go home?"

"I..." I snap my mouth shut and swallow hard.

We have to be out of the vacation rental on Monday. The kids will be starting school soon, and I need to get my tutoring students scheduled for the fall semester.

"I like it here. So does Teddy. Even Declan..." Her voice fades off and Teddy groans as he settles next to her.

"I like it too," I whisper.

Not only has it been nice to be close to my best friend again, but I like the slower pace. The speed of Aspen Falls is less intense than the pace back home.

And Jagger.

He plays into the equation now.

He helped me get Maisie inside before running next door to change. But we still need to talk.

We both want this to work, but what would that look like with him here and me there?

Can I trust that he won't revert back to the playboy he was when we got here? Or am I only setting myself—and my kids—up for heartbreak later? We had talked about making this something more, but I never walked into this with that intent.

I'm used to reading about instalove. But suddenly I'm living that trope.

It's hard to trust it, but I want to.

Anticipation and anxiety fizz through my blood. Sitting still and waiting for him?

My jittery nerves don't think so.

Sighing, I rub Teddy's head.

"Keep an eye on her," I murmur.

He lets out a soft snort of affirmation before resting his head on his paws.

I head to Declan's room next. I knock, and when he calls out, I push the door open. He's lying in bed in basketball shorts and a T-shirt, his eyes glued to the phone in his hand.

"Hey, buddy, I'll be right back, okay? I'm going to run next door."

Declan side-eyes me briefly before homing in on his phone screen again. "'Kay."

Still dressed in my bridesmaid's dress from the wedding, I head for Jagger's. I don't want to waste the time it would take for me to change. So, barefoot, I cross the yard. The grass is dry beneath my feet, though it's somewhat soft and cool despite the summer heat. Once the sun goes down here, the temperature does drop quickly. As evidenced by the goose bumps that dot my bare arms as I take the two steps to his porch.

I knock and wait, but after several breaths, there's no sign of him. I try again, this time twisting the knob—unlocked— as I knock on the door.

"Jagger?" I call, but I don't get a response.

His shoes are kicked off by the front door and his keys are on the table next to it.

"Maybe upstairs?" I guess, trailing my fingers up the banister lightly as I make my way to the second floor.

His bedroom door is closed, but another door is open. Maybe he's in here?

"Jagger?" I push open the door and discover bookshelves lining each wall with multiple copies of books.

*The Reality of Love* by JA Hart.

Another shelf is full of *Lovers and Friends*.

An entire bookcase is dedicated to the Compass series. The one that was on my reading list until I read *The Reality of Love*.

Every single book in this room is by JA Hart.

"Jagger is…"

I turn slowly, taking in the scene. All the prettily arranged paperbacks that in any other circumstance I might consider heaven. But the man I've been falling for, the one who told me he wanted to make this work, is…

"JA Hart," I say out loud as I trace one of the spines.

He admitted to being a romance author.

But never which one.

*You didn't ask.*

Touché.

I should go. There's a reason he keeps this door closed. Maybe he was going to tell me. And then I would tell him, gently, that I read *The Reality of Love* and didn't like it.

I need to get out of here.

As I turn toward the door, my attention catches on the two monitors lit up on the desk.

Dread cramps my stomach as I step closer and read the words on the screen.

"A little about me. I'm a single mom to two kids and coordinate their chaos in Colorado. We recently added a Tasmanian devil of a goldendoodle puppy…"

The familiar swirl of pinks and browns that coordinate with the brand I created border the screen where a picture of Teddy—midchew on an expensive leather boot of mine—stares back at me.

Does he realize that I'm Rocky Mountain Romance Reader?

I force my attention away from the photo and focus on the second monitor.

Pulled up there is an email to Jagger from Kim Davis, his editor based on her signature line.

*Jagger,*

*Take a breath. If authors went after every blogger who gave them a negative review, there would be no bloggers left. I do not recommend trying to shut down her blog like you mentioned. So what if you're not her cup of tea? No author can please every reader. Just forget her and move on. Do not, and I repeat, do not comment on her blog post.*
*Kim*
*P.S. Where's your manuscript? You're late.*

"Hayley?"

I jump and whirl around at the sound of Jagger's voice. He's standing in the doorway, his hair damp and the dark-blue cotton of his T-shirt clinging to him in damp patches that highlight a muscular chest I've traced with my fingers and lips.

"S-sorry. I came over since you've been gone longer than I thought you would be. I saw this door was open and…"

And what?

And I know the truth?

Apparently so does he.

"I got distracted." His face shutters, and all traces of emotion vanish from his expression.

"You know who I am?" I gesture toward the screen.

He nods and steps into the room, crossing his arms over his chest. "Not until tonight. When you mentioned you had a blog, I got this…feeling…in the pit of my stomach. I figured it was worth checking out."

"Which is why you didn't come right back."

It's a guess, but he nods again.

"You want to shut down my blog?" The initial shock that hit me is starting to give way to anger.

Like his editor said, who cares if I didn't like his book?

"I…was pretty pissed off when I read your review of *The Reality of Love*." He frowns. "You two-starred me."

"And?" I cross my arms over my chest, mimicking his stance.

"I worked hard on that book, and you acted like it was trash." A muscle tics in his jaw.

I swear I can feel my blood pressure rising. "I never said it was trash!"

"No, instead you just questioned my ability to 'please a woman–be they reader or lover.'" He spits the words out, a direct quote from my post.

I flinch. Shit. I'd forgotten that part. In my defense, I'd had a particularly rough day with Declan and was cursing Rob more than normal. But that wasn't Jagger's fault.

"I…"

His face twists into the smirk that greeted me that first day and he steps closer, close enough that the smell of his body wash wraps around me. Only now it's not a comforting scent the way I've come to associate it.

"But now, gorgeous, I think you and I can both agree that I know how to please a woman, can't we?"

It's like the last few weeks haven't happened. He's the same person I met that first time when I fell at his feet. My heart plummets, and my fingers itch with the desire to slap that smirk off his face.

Is he really that good of an actor? Or was he only hiding who he really was to get what he wanted? Based on what I learned from my ex, I can't give Jagger any benefit of the doubt.

"You're an asshole." Gritting my teeth, I push past him.

He grasps my wrist to stop me, and when I turn back, regret lines his face, and his eyes are remorseful.

"Hayls, I'm sorry."

I swallow down the anger bubbling up inside me. "Yeah, that makes two of us."

Yanking my hand free, I step back, crossing the threshold into the hallway.

"Hayley."

Tears burn my nose and behind my eyes. I don't bother to try to hide them.

This fucking hurts. More than the ending of my marriage.

Which is ridiculous.

I was married for twelve years. Jagger and I have been together for two weeks. And the thing between us was casual... until it wasn't.

And now it's nothing at all.

"I can't do this right now," I say and head for the stairs.

"Hayley." He follows me, but stops halfway down the steps.

My hand is already on the knob.

"I..." He snaps his mouth shut. The writer. At a loss for words.

"Maybe this is a sign," I tell him.

The frown he gives me is full of pain and confusion. "A sign?"

"From the universe. We wanted to make this work, but maybe it's not supposed to."

"Maybe it is," he tells me, taking two more steps closer.

"I...don't know. I need some time to think."

"You leave on Monday."

It's a reminder I don't need. "I know."

"What does that mean?" he asks.

"I don't know."

"Will I see you before you leave?"

I don't have an answer for that question either.

*Do you have an answer for anything?*

I give him the only answer I have for right now.

"Goodbye, Jagger."

# CHAPTER 17

## JAGGER

*"You're an idiot," Tom says, giving me a pointed look that reinforces his statement.*
*It's one I've seen hundreds of times. Thousands.*
*"Why am I an idiot?" I prop my hands on my hips and wait for his answer.*
*"You love her, you idiot. But you're letting her walk away."*
*It hits a little too close to home, but I laugh it off.*
*"Who says I love her?"*
*"Sam, I've known you since we were catching ladybugs in our backyards. I've seen you with Rose. I've seen you with her kids. Anyone who knows you can tell that you're in love with her. With them."*

"*F*uck."

I push back from my desk and drop my head back against my chair.

Tom is a combination of Shep and Shep's Uncle Joe. Both in appearance and mannerisms and the tell-it-like-it-is-take-no-shit attitude.

Uncle Joe's voice is the one ringing through the room now,

calling me twelve different kinds of fool for letting Hayley leave. No, even worse. For getting pissed off to begin with.

Who the fuck cares that she's Rocky Mountain Romance Reader? Or that she didn't like *The Reality of Love*?

Does it change my reality? Does it negate the way I've fallen for her? The way I've fallen for her kids?

No, the fuck it does not.

Shoving free of my desk chair, I pace to the window and stare out across the dark night to the dimly lit house next door. It's late, I'm sure everyone is in bed. The only lights on are probably the one above the stove and one in the hall in case one of the kids has to go to the bathroom.

"You fucked up, Brooks," I say aloud. I turn from the window only to pace back after several steps.

Is Hayley still awake?

I shouldn't go over there.

*Yes, the fuck you should.*

It's as if Uncle Joe is in the room with me.

"She's pissed at me."

She has every right to be.

She read that email right next to the page I had pulled up. After she mentioned being a blogger, I had a gut feeling that she was Rocky Mountain Romance Reader. I spent hours on her blog after reading her review, figuring out which books she liked, which she didn't—there weren't many—and wondering what it was about her that made her dislike my book as much as she did.

Her bio mentioned that she was a single mom. I assumed that meant the blogger was divorced. So I wondered if she disliked the book because it was written by a male romance author. But, no, she five-starred a book by a different male romance author not long before reading mine. And her review made me want to spend what little free time I have checking out his book.

*Why don't you ask her why she didn't like it—why she had said what she did?*

"Because that would have been rational, and my go-to is apparently defensive asshole."

Granted, it didn't take me long to figure that out. I didn't need the character of Tom operating as my imaginary Shep and Uncle Joe combined. The words on the page just reinforced what I already knew—I had fucked up.

And I knew what happened when the male main character fucked it up. But what kind of grand gesture should I plan? The cursor on my computer screen blinks, the off and on slowly morphing to a morse code.

Fingers hovering over my keyboard, I know what I have to do. With one keystroke followed by another, the story pours onto the page. Everything I'm feeling, our entire story—from our meet-cute, when she fell at my feet, through my asshole defensiveness that pushed her away—it's all there. Including the ending I want.

The sun is peeking above the horizon when I stumble from my porch with a thick manila envelope clutched in my hands like I'm terrified a rogue wind is going to come from nowhere and scatter the pages I'd printed out after I typed the two words every writer loves. *The End*. But not for Hayley and me. Or for Declan and Maisie. I hope this is still our beginning.

The sky is a peachy shade of pink with swirls of purple and blue as the sun continues to climb, but I focus on putting one foot in front of the other until I'm standing at her door. I lift my hand, both tempted and hesitant to knock. The desire to play my version of ding-dong-ditch pushes at my limbs, urging me to drop the envelope and run.

"Quit being a chicken and knock on the fucking door."

The sooner I deliver this, the sooner I can sink into the anxiety that'll plague me while I wait, wondering whether she's reading it, whether she likes it. Maybe I'll even get more than the fifteen minutes of sleep I got in my desk chair as I waited for the manuscript to print.

But despite my demand, I don't knock. No, I stand there, a combination of hesitation and hope paralyzing me until the door swings inward. Hayley stands so she's mostly hidden behind the door. A sleep shirt grazes the hem of her shorts that display her legs in all their sun-kissed glory. I swallow around the lump of words that sit on my windpipe and force my focus back to her face.

"What are you doing here?" she asks.

I curse myself for causing the wariness that pinches her eyes and lips. The look is so unnatural. It's a reminder of how far we've come in such a short time. I know all her expressions. From the pissed-off look she gave me when she glared at me from my front porch to the hesitant smile at Shep and Jade's when I had apologized to her and Maisie. The soft smile as we talked by her firepit the first night I kissed her. The pleasure that tinted her cheeks rosy and softened her lips as she breathed my name. The tears that shimmered in her eyes when she watched me dance with Maisie at the wedding. Until last night when all those emotions had drained and left behind the cautious expression she's wearing now.

"I, um, here." I thrust the envelope at her and remind myself to let go when she takes it from me.

"What's this?"

I take a deep breath and rush through an explanation.

"You don't owe me anything. I was an asshole and I'd absolutely deserve it if you told me to fuck off and slammed the door in my face. But I'm hoping that, even if you do, you'll read what's in the envelope."

Her grip on the door tightens, and for a heartbeat I'm worried she's going to do exactly like I just said and slam the door in my face. God knows I deserve it.

"Please?" I trace her knuckles with my index finger.

By some miracle, she doesn't pull away. But there's a war waging in her dark brown eyes—the same flare of hope that burns in my chest battering against the walls she's so desperately trying to keep in place.

"Why?"

Well, fuck.

*You didn't expect that question, did you, dumbass?*

I open my mouth and close it again as I try to find the words. They're so much easier on paper.

*Try, dipshit. Before you lose her completely.*

"I fucked up. And the words come better for me in written form than spoken. I think we both understand what a fucking idiot I am when I speak. I'm hoping that"—I point to the envelope still clutched in her hand—"is enough to explain what I wish I could verbalize. It's a poor excuse, that I'll only put my foot in my mouth, but I don't want to fuck it up again. I'm sorry. I reacted…"

"Like an asshole?" she supplies.

My heart squeezes painfully. "Exactly. And I don't want to be that guy, Hayley. Not with you. Not with Maisie or Declan. You guys deserve so much better than my worst, and my worst is what you got last night. You make me want to be a better man. For all of you. To be the hero of your story, instead of the villain. You deserve him."

I point at the envelope again.

"I want to be him. If you'll let me."

In response, she only studies me silently.

My heart sinks into my stomach. "Just please read it before you decide. I have no right to ask you anything, but…just read it. If you want to give me another chance, I'll be waiting."

I brush my finger against hers again and step back. Then I force myself to retreat down the stairs and watch her close the door without a backward glance.

*Now what?*

"Now, we wait."

Wait. And hope.

# CHAPTER 18

## HAYLEY

*T*o say that I had not expected to find Jagger standing outside my door with his hand raised to knock when I woke up this morning would be an understatement.

Part of me wanted to say no.

*Liar. You're intrigued.*

I am. The envelope is thick and heavy. Rather than rip it open, I set it on the kitchen table and do my best to ignore the manila beacon while I brew and pour a cup of coffee and doctor it with the appropriate level of creamer I need to get through the day.

Newsflash. It's a lot more than normal given the roller coaster of the last twenty-four hours.

Only after I've taken the first sip do I make my way to the table with all the excitement of a death-row inmate heading toward an electric chair. Setting my coffee cup off to the side, I flip over the envelope. And with a deep breath in, I undo the clasp and slip the stack of papers out. The topmost sheet is a letter with my name on it.

*Dear Hayley,*

Never in a million years did I picture you walking into my life. I thought I was happy living my life the way I always had. Until you. You, Declan, and Maisie have shown me that what I was doing before wasn't living. Or maybe it was but only halfway. With you, because of you, I realize what it's like to have a full life. To find joy in simple pleasures like family movie night, a day at the lake, the sound of the kids playing with the dog.

I meant what I said when I told you I wanted to make this work. Then I went and acted like a jackass, pretended as though there was nothing between us when that couldn't be further from the truth. You have no idea how sorry I am about that. If I could do it over, I would. But I wouldn't change meeting you or falling for you as hard and as fast as I did.

The first book I ever wrote was inspired by a story my sister, Brittany, told me about a weekend trip she took to Vegas with her best friend. I thought that book was easy to write. Until I wrote this story. This one poured out of me like nothing has before. This is our story. One I hope has a happy ending.

I'll be waiting.

All my love,

Jagger

Tears line my lashes, and before I can stop them, they spill over and drop to the page I'm holding. My hands shake as I set it facedown next to the bigger stack of paper. I wipe my tears with the back of my wrist and pick up the top page.

*Falling for the Woman Next Door*. A novel by JA Hart.

The next page has a dedication that has the tears burning behind my eyes again.

For Hayley. For all our tomorrows.

With a deep breath, I flip the page.

"Chapter one…"

Hours later, after taking a break to feed the kids breakfast, then curling up on the couch with the manuscript, I read the last words.

*"You're what I've always been afraid to want, Rose. But I don't want to lose you. To lose us. I'm more afraid to lose you than to love you."*

*"You aren't going to lose me, Sam. I love you."*

*"Fuck, I love you too." I pull her to me and crush my lips to hers, loving how her fingernails prick into the backs of my arms.*

*"Now what?" she says, tilting her head back to allow me to explore the line of her jaw with my lips.*

*"Now we get to find our forever." My lips find hers, and it's only when my body demands oxygen that I break the connection.*

*"I love you," she murmurs.*

*And I'll never get tired of hearing those words from her lips.*

*"Forever."*

*The End*

Blinking, I bring the room back into focus.

"Holy shit," I breathe.

It's like I've just gotten back from a different world. I guess, in a way, I have. I've been immersed in Sam and Rose's world, watching the grumpy playboy next door fall in love with the single mom with two kids.

It was our story. Mine and Jagger's.

Wrapped up in a work of fiction.

An amazing work of fiction.

How did Jagger write both *The Reality of Love* and *Falling for the Woman Next Door*? The books are vastly different. This one had me turning pages and falling more and more into the story whereas I considered DNFing the other more than once.

"Mom?" Declan stands in the doorway, his phone nowhere in sight for the first time since he got the thing last year.

"Yeah, buddy?"

"Are you sick?"

"No, why do you say that?"

"You've been inside all morning."

"I have?"

"Yeah."

"Where's Maisie?"

He thumbs toward the window. "She's outside playing with Teddy."

"Oh. Are you guys hungry? Ready for lunch?"

I unfold from the couch and my legs twinge after being in the same position for so long. Declan was right, I have been in here for a while.

He shrugs. "I guess."

I meet him in the doorway and squeeze him in a one-armed hug. "You okay, buddy?"

He's quiet as I follow him into the kitchen, and he heads for the refrigerator to grab what's left of the lunch meat I bought last week.

His head is buried in the appliance when he finally responds. "If you wanted to stay here, I'd be okay with that."

It takes me several heartbeats to process his muffled words. "You want to stay here?" I prop myself up against the counter to wait for his response.

He turns around and sets out the lunch meat, cheese, and

mustard. Then he mimics my stance, leaning against the opposite counter.

"It'd be okay. I like hanging out with Shep and Jade. And Jagger. He's pretty cool."

"You think so?" I ask, feigning way more indifference than what's actually coursing through my body.

What I do next hinges on Declan's response.

"Yeah. At first I didn't think so. He was mean to Maisie and Teddy. But then he hung around us more and I don't know. Relaxed, I guess? But it's like he wants to be around us. Not like…"

My heart cracks a little at the hurt that flashes across his face. "Not like your dad," I finish softly.

There's so much pain deep in my son's eyes. I want to close the distance and pull him into a hug. But he wouldn't want that. And it wouldn't change the complicated mess of emotions Rob's treatment of Declan has created. Part of me is ecstatic that Maisie is too young to understand.

Declan clears his throat. "I'm just saying. If you wanted to stay here, it'd be okay."

It doesn't sound like any of us is ready to leave Aspen Falls anytime soon.

"Okay, bud. I appreciate that. You want to go tell Maisie it's time for lunch?"

"Yeah." He pushes away from the counter in a blur of gangly arms and legs as he goes to get his sister.

In the last twenty-four hours, both of my children have asked if we're going to stay here. They've given me their approval— even in a roundabout way—to upend our lives again. Yesterday, when Maisie asked, the answer had been simple. I wanted to stay too. I didn't want to leave Jade…or Jagger. But then last night happened and I went to bed with plans to pack up and go home.

And then Jagger gave me his story.

Before I make any decisions, I need to talk to him.

*I'll be waiting.*

That's what his letter said.

"Mooommy, I'm hungry." Maisie's voice is echoed by the slam of the screen door.

First priority—feed my kids.

A close second?

Talk to Jagger.

# CHAPTER 19

## JAGGER

*I* don't sleep when I get home—I pass out.

After the events of last night, it's hard to believe that only twenty-four hours ago I watched my best friend marry his soulmate.

Between the wedding festivities, the argument with Hayley, and then staying up all night to finish the story, there was no way I'd stay awake. My body demanded I sleep. But only a few hours later, my mind woke me up and anxiety drove me from my bed and kept me pacing the length of my kitchen. Every so often, I stopped at the window to stare at Hayley's house.

Maisie came outside with Teddy, giggling as the puppy ran circles around her and barked. I couldn't help but smile as I watched them, even as my heart ached. They're leaving tomorrow and my own stupid actions were keeping me from spending what little time they had left here with them.

"Your. Own. Stupid. Fault," I mutter, turning from the window.

There haven't been any signs of Declan. Or Hayley.

I force myself to trudge up the stairs. I need a shower. Every part of me feels as though I ran a marathon yesterday. I'm not in my twenties anymore, so the lack of a good night's sleep is wreaking havoc on both my body and my ability to think clearly.

The hot water is heaven on my sore shoulders. I stand under the stream for what could be two minutes or twenty, zoned out, before I go through the motions of washing my hair and my body.

Finished with the shower, I crank the water off and step out. I'm wrapping a towel around my waist when the sound of a knock reaches me. With suddenly trembling hands, I secure a knot in the cloth at my hip and race downstairs, terrified that she'll leave before I get to the door.

How do I know it's her?

The same way I knew she was Rocky Mountain Romance Reader.

I just do.

"I'm coming, I'm coming. Don't leave," I call out. I push my wet hair out of my face as I take the stairs as quickly as I can.

The last thing I need to do is miss a step and break my neck. Miraculously, I make it to the door in one piece and throw it open to a surprised Hayley.

"Hi." I'm breathing heavy, but try to hide it as best I can.

"Can I come in?" Though her lip quivers, she smiles. That alone fans the ember of hope that's kept me going.

"Fuck, I'm sorry. Yes, of course, come on in."

I step to the side and usher her in, breathing in deeply as she passes me, desperate to get a hit of her fresh-baked snickerdoodle scent. It may be the last time I get the chance, so I'm taking advantage of the opportunity.

I close the door and we stand awkwardly at the bottom of the stairs. I'm not sure where to start.

What happened to the smooth man who never struggled with what to say to women? Oh, yeah, he fell in love and turned into a bumbling idiot.

*You could ask her if she read the book, dumbass.*

"Did you..."

When her eyes dip to my chest, I follow the movement, only now realizing I'm wearing nothing but a towel. Two weeks ago, I would have made a flirty quip about always answering the door in my towel. Two days ago, I would have crowded her against the wall and kissed her until neither of us cared about the towel or clothes.

But we're not the same people we were then, so I grip the knot and lift a hand.

"Shit. Give me a minute to go get dressed."

She nods. "Okay."

"You won't leave?" My stomach twists, but I need to make sure.

She lowers her chin and shakes her head subtly. "No."

Relief floods me but it doesn't stop me from taking the stairs two at a time and throwing on a pair of shorts and T-shirt at a world-record speed. When I leave my room and head down the stairs, she isn't waiting where I left her.

My heart stutters, and my voice is strangled by emotion when I call her name.

"Hayley?"

She steps into the doorway of the kitchen, backlit by the sunlight filtering in through the windows, and the universe clicks back into place.

"I'm here."

I attempt to hide my sigh as the grip of panic that squeezed my heart releases, but my relief is too potent.

"Thanks for waiting. I was getting out of the shower when I heard your knock. I didn't want to miss you."

I close the distance between us and pull up short, even though all I want to do is wrap my arms around her and bury my face in her hair.

Her chest rises and falls with the rapid breath she sucks in and releases. "How did you know it was me?" She turns away and heads for two mugs set out on the counter.

I take the one she holds out to me and sip the dark nectar of life. "I hoped it was you." I can't explain it, but my gut told me it was her.

She takes a sip of her own coffee and leans against the opposite counter. I hate the kitchen island between us, but closing the distance won't resolve the emotional break we've suffered.

After several heartbeats go by with the two of us staring at each other and drinking coffee, I finally work up the courage to ask, "Did you read it?"

She gives me a small nod and studies the coffee in her cup. "I did."

When she doesn't elaborate, imposter syndrome rears its ugly head.

Did she hate it as much as she did *The Reality of Love*?

"And?" I ask, bracing myself for her response.

*Quit being so dramatic. If she hated it, would she be here right now?*

She presses her teeth into the plump flesh of her lower lip. "Did you mean it?"

Her question catches me off guard. Blinking, I tilt my head to one side. "Mean what?"

"That you wrote our story. That you want *the* happily ever after."

Distance be damned. I circle the island and gently pry her coffee from her hand. Once I've set it on the counter, I weave my fingers with hers.

"It is absolutely what I mean. I'm so fucking sorry that I was a dick last night. You didn't deserve that. At all. That was my own insecurity coming out to play."

"You were going to try to shut down my blog," she says, eyes locked on mine, the accusation clear.

I nod. "You're right. I did."

She drops her chin and tries to tug her hands free, but I squeeze her fingers with mine.

"I'm not going to lie about it. Was it a mature decision? Not even close. Your review hurt. But it was true. I forced things in that book, and I shouldn't have. Everything you said was true. I didn't want to face the honesty. You only got one thing wrong."

Her hands relax in mine, and her breathing shallows as she tilts her chin and locks eyes with me.

"What?" Her voice has taken on the breathy quality I love.

But let's face it. I love her voice regardless.

I love all of her.

"You tell me," I say, reeling her forward until her body is pressed to mine.

Her breath catches and her pupils dilate, eclipsing the warm brown with something hotter.

"Oh."

I'm captivated by the way her lips form that single word, ready to dive in and savor it on her lips, but we're not done talking.

"Yes, 'oh.' But what I want to improve on is words—"

"You are good with words. What I read—"

"I meant with you, Hayls. Words like *I'm sorry*. Words like *I'm in awe of you*. Of the strength and the grace you show to everyone around you. How well you're raising two of the best kids I've ever met—"

"You haven't met that many kids."

Fuck, the sassy tilt of her lips is making it difficult to concentrate on anything but kissing her.

"Words like I love you," I blurt out.

Those three words hang between us, shimmering in the silence.

She swallows thickly and searches my face. "You love me?"

"Yes. Fuck, I didn't mean to drop them like that. I wanted to spend more time groveling, but I couldn't stop the words from coming out, just like I couldn't stop myself from falling. I don't care if you two-star every book I ever write. Fuck, one-star me for all I care, but it's not going to change the fact that I love you. I love you and Declan, Maisie, and even Teddy. I can't go back to living the way I did before you fell into my life—literally."

Her smile matches my own. "You want me to one-star you?" she asks with a shake of her head.

"Baby, I don't care how you rate my writing, so long as you give me five stars for loving you. Those are the only stars I care about."

"I think I can do that."

"You think?" I ask with a squeeze of my arms around her.

She gasps as I pull her in so we're chest to chest. "I also think you need to kiss me." With a smirk, she pops up on her tiptoes to bring her mouth close to mine.

"And why is that?" My lips brush hers with my words.

"Because I love you too."

She closes the distance and winds her arms around my neck, fusing our mouths and tangling her tongue with mine. With a groan, I take control of the kiss, gripping her waist and lifting her onto the counter. Stepping between her legs, I roam the soft skin of her inner thighs and tease her beneath the hem of her shorts.

She squirms against the counter and wraps her legs around my waist, pulling me closer.

I break the kiss, trailing my lips along her jaw to her ear. "Where are the kids?"

"Watching a movie at my house."

"How long do we have?" I sink my teeth into her earlobe and tug.

She moans, tilting her head to give me better access. "Long enough."

That's not true.

Even if I had forever with this woman, it wouldn't be long enough.

# EPILOGUE

## HAYLEY

*T*he sun isn't even above the horizon when I wake up the next morning. Jagger is pressed against my back with one leg tossed over mine and one arm holding me snugly against his chest. His even breaths ruffle the small hairs at my nape. I'd love to close my eyes and drift back to sleep, but my mind is whirring with memories of the last forty-eight hours and plans for the trip back to the Springs I have to take this afternoon.

I don't want to leave, but if I want to move up here permanently, then I need to head back and start getting things ready. While Jagger and I work out the details, the kids will have to start school. I'll continue tutoring, taking the few college courses I needed, and my blog. Having it all means less time for tutoring, but I'm ready to move forward and that includes finishing my teaching degree so I can find a job in Aspen Falls.

I wiggle my hips back against Jagger, and in response, he slides a hand to my breast and squeezes. But then he shifts and rolls over onto his other side.

Okay, then.

I lie where I am and close my eyes, but there's no way I can fall back asleep. Frustrated, I toss back the covers and head for the bathroom. When I'm finished, I pad downstairs and start coffee. While I wait, I spy my laptop sitting on the dining room table where it's been for the last two days.

I lift the lid and pull up my blog. When my coffee is finished, I sit and click on the link for a new post. I'm still in that same position, wholly absorbed in my work, when a warm arm wraps around my shoulder and skilled lips press a kiss to the back of my neck.

"G'morning," he murmurs.

I squeeze his arm where it rests along my collarbone and lean against him.

"Good morning."

"I woke up and you were gone."

"Couldn't sleep." I tilt my head back for the chaste kiss he presses against my mouth.

"How long have you been up?" Releasing me, he steps back and scrubs a hand down his face.

I peek at the clock and immediately have to do a double take. "Wow, I guess about an hour or so?"

He pours himself a cup of coffee and sits next to me at the table. "Whatcha been up to?" he asks and nods his head toward my laptop.

"A post."

Wariness flashes in his expression, but just as quickly his eyes shift to curious. "About?"

"You," I tell him.

He brings his coffee cup to his lips, but not quick enough to hide his grimace.

"Trust me?"

This is a big step, but his response will tell me whether he really meant what he said. Is he really over my review of *The Reality of Love?*

He dips his chin. "I trust you, Hayls."

"Here." I turn my laptop toward him and pick up my luke-warm coffee.

"*Summer is drawing to an end, my bookish friends,*" he reads, "*and I'm still attacking my TBR with all the gusto that the single-mom life can handle. I wanted to let you all in on something. I may have been wrong to judge JA Hart on* The Reality of Love. *Okay, I was definitely wrong. I recently read something that I'm hoping he'll release sooner rather than later. Let me tell you—you'll want to read this one. Five stars. More than five if it were possible. What's the name of this swoon masterpiece? It's called* Falling for the Woman Next Door. *You'll have to excuse this recommendation because it's based on a true story. My true story. With author JA Hart. My next-door neighbor for the summer.*"

He stops and looks at me, a smile tugging at the corner of his lips.

"More than five stars, huh?"

I gesture toward the computer. "Keep reading."

He focuses back on the screen. "*P.S. You know how in my last blog about JA, I made an assumption about his prowess? I'm happy to report I couldn't have been more wrong. Stay sexy, my bookish friend. I'll catch you at the end of my next read.*"

"What do you think?"

"You published this?"

I nod.

"Even this PS?"

"I'm not ashamed to admit I was wrong."

He leans closer, his eyes heating, and grips the back of my neck to bring me closer.

"Have I told you that I love you?" he murmurs.

"Not today," I tell him.

"I love you."

Warmth floods my stomach and happiness fizzes through my body.

"I love you too."

He closes the distance between us, his mouth leisurely exploring mine. Teasing kisses from one side to the other, then tracing the seam of my lips with his tongue—a request I grant, eagerly, so I can enjoy the sensation of his tongue against mine.

Without breaking our connection, I shift until I'm straddling his lap. I want more. So much more. But the kitchen is not the best place for this.

"Maybe we should go back upstairs," I whisper.

He traces hot, open-mouthed kisses down my neck, pulling a mewl from me.

"That was my plan when I woke up," he growls against my skin.

He stands and lifts me in his arms, and I wrap my legs around his waist.

"Mooooom!" The sound of Maisie calling for me is accompanied by the scurried click of Teddy's nails against the floor.

With a groan, Jagger releases my hips, and I slide down until my feet are planted on the floor.

"We'll have to continue this chapter later," I tell him.

"There's no doubt we'll be picking this up later."

One of the best parts about dating a writer? He's good at planning out the next chapter. And he makes sure we both get our happily ever after.

THE END

---

LOVE JAGGER'S LOVE STORY WITH SINGLE MOM HAYLEY? Jagger's sister, Brittany is about to be a single mom too. Or is she? Check out her enemies to lovers/enemies with benefits, rock star, best friend's older sibling happily ever after, ONE WEEKEND IN VEGAS. Keep reading for a sneak peek!

Want more of Hayley and Jagger? Turn the page to see what life is like for them on moving day!

# BONUS EPILOGUE

## JAGGER

ALMOST ONE YEAR LATER

"*I* don't know who's more excited. You or the kids," Hayley says to me from the driver's seat of her Subaru as we approach the turn for the house.

I poke her side, and with a giggle, she squirms away.

"I think you're just as excited about finally moving in."

We didn't anticipate that this process would take so long. But between Hayley's schoolwork and the sale of her house in Colorado Springs—and her ex's decision to be an asshole about it —and the renovations on my house, there's no way we could have gotten to this point sooner.

Hayley makes the turn, and in the side mirror, I catch a glimpse of the U-Haul that Shep drives bumping along behind us.

"We're almost there!" Maisie squeals.

Hayley and I share a smile and Teddy barks his agreement.

Even Declan takes his headphones off and tucks both them and his phone away.

"I can't wait to see my new room," Maisie continues to chatter in the backseat. "And Teddy's going to sleep with me every night. So it's like he and I are sharing a room."

When the house becomes visible through the trees, Hayley slows to a stop.

"Oh, Jagger."

Even the outside has changed. The wide front porch is still there, but it now wraps around the two-story addition that includes two extra bedrooms, a full bathroom, and dedicated office space.

Hayley knew about the renovations, obviously, and helped me choose paint colors and flooring, but she hasn't seen the addition. I wanted it to be a surprise.

"Do you like it?"

Nerves dance with the excitement inside me. Fuck. I hope they love it. My family is here. Finally.

Because that's what Hayley, Declan, and Maisie are.

My family.

"I-I love it."

The smile on her face when she turns to me demands that I kiss her. Just a chaste brush of my lips against hers given the audience in the backseat and the sharp horn blast from Shep.

"Get a room," he yells.

"Ew." Declan shudders.

She eases the car down the road and pulls in, leaving space for Shep to back the truck up so we can unload the boxes and the few pieces of furniture Hayley wanted from their house. Everything else is already set up in the kids' rooms.

"You want the tour?" I ask as Maisie scrambles from the backseat with Teddy hot on her heels.

"Can I go see my room?" Declan asks.

I twist in the seat until I can meet his gaze. "This is your house now, too, bud. You don't have to ask to do things." Hayley shoots me a look and I amend my statement. "Within reason."

Declan rolls his eyes like any good teen boy would and climbs out. I follow and wave at Shep.

"I'm going to show Hayley and the kids," I shout.

"Take your time. Jade and I are going to take a quick walk to stretch our legs."

At the door, Maisie, Declan, and Teddy are waiting. I key in the code and turn the knob, and then the kids are off, rushing through the house.

"Welcome home," I murmur to Hayley.

She turns toward me and throws her arms around my neck. We stand in the doorway holding each other as happy exclamations from the kids echo around us.

"I bet you're glad you don't have to drive down to the Springs every weekend anymore," she says.

Rather than alternating weekends with her, I chose to drive down to avoid disrupting the kids' lives. It meant promoting Becky to my manager and hiring more help for the Expedition, but it's been well worth it.

"I wish it had been every weekend. I hated being away from you for so long when the snow was bad."

"We made it work. And you got more material for your next book," she teases.

"Phone sex is nowhere near as satisfying as holding you." I tighten my arms to prove my point.

"It's a good thing we don't have to worry about that anymore."

"You ready for your tour?"

"More than ready." She lifts onto her tiptoes and brushes a kiss on my chin.

Hours later, the kids and Hayley have had their tours, Shep and I have unloaded the U-Haul, and Hayley and Jade have made good progress on the mountain of boxes. Shep and Jade left after dinner with promises to return the U-Haul to the rental place tomorrow so we can continue to work on unpacking.

"It's quiet," I tell Hayley as we put away the last few items in the kitchen.

"Almost too quiet. I'm going to go check on the kids."

As she leaves, I fold up the box and stack it next to the door. Then I flip off lights and head upstairs to find my family. Hayley is standing in Maisie's doorway.

Quietly, I come up behind her and rest my chin on her hair. Maisie is passed out sideways in her bed, and Teddy is sprawled next to her. Maisie is still in her clothes from earlier, and her hair is a tangled mass around her head.

"She's exhausted," I whisper.

"It's been a big day. I should move her so she doesn't fall off," Hayley murmurs back.

"I'll do it. Did you check on Declan?"

She shakes her head. "Not yet."

"Meet you in our room in five minutes?"

"Okay."

As I shift Maisie to a normal sleeping position, Teddy doesn't move, but he acknowledges my presence with a thump of his tail against the blankets.

"Goodnight, Maisie." The words are quiet as I pull the blankets into position.

I make sure the nightlight in her room, as well as the one in the kids' bathroom, is on before making my way down the hall to my bedroom—our bedroom. Hayley is already in there, standing at the windows that overlook the lake.

"Declan okay?" I close the distance, unable to keep from tucking an arm around her. She's here. In reality and not just in my dreams.

She doesn't turn from the windows. "He was already asleep too."

"Are you tired?" I ask.

"Not quite." She rotates in my hold and loops her arms around my neck.

176

"Did you have something in mind?" I tease her, lowering my head until my lips are millimeters from hers.

"Maybe."

"And what might that be, Hayls?"

"I was thinking we should christen our new bed."

"It is our first night here together." I swoop down and catch an arm behind her knees, then lift her bridal style.

Her mouth connects with mine and I moan at her flavor.

Mine.

And sooner rather than later I'll make it official. I've already talked to Declan and he's on board. I haven't said much to Maisie, though, since I doubt the little girl can keep a secret.

I make it to the bed and have just lowered her to the purple and teal bedspread when a knock echoes up the stairs. The skid of Teddy's paws on the floor is accompanied by the Cujo-sounding bark as he tears down the stairs.

"Fuck. Who the hell could that be?"

I follow, shushing the dog and hoping he doesn't wake the kids up. Hayley is right behind me, and she grabs his collar while I open the door.

"Britt?"

My sister stands on my porch, a small suitcase gripped in one hand. I take it from her and tug her inside.

Teddy sniffs my sister once before heading back upstairs. Some guard dog he is.

"What the hell are you doing here so late? Did you drive from Denver tonight?" I ask her.

"I-I didn't know where else to go," she says.

"You're welcome here anytime," I tell her.

Beside me, Hayley nods in confirmation.

"Do you want something to drink? Water, coffee? I've got beer in the—"

"How about a place to live and a job?" she asks. "I'm pregnant."

Announcement made, she bursts into tears.

# ONE WEEKEND IN VEGAS

## BRITTANY

$\mathcal{F}$ifteen dollars changed my life.

Well, fifteen dollars and the countless orgasms gifted to me by my best friend's older brother.

Or maybe it was the two blue lines in a little window of the fifteen-dollar pregnancy test...

"Hello, earth to Brittany," my best friend, Krista, says from beside the king-size bed in our hotel room. "Are you going to stand in the doorway for the whole weekend, or did you want to come in?"

I maneuver my carry-on through the door and nearly trip over it as it catches on the carpet.

"There's only one bed."

We've shared a bed before. Plenty of times. We've been best friends since we were eight years old. But we always get two queen beds on our girls' trip weekends.

The weekends that are going to be very limited in the foreseeable future.

"I told Ryder I didn't care. You never use your bed anyway." With a saucy wink at me, she parks her small suitcase on one side of the bed.

"You told your brother that?" My pitch is so high I'm sure only dogs can hear me as I finish the question.

"Chill. It's not like he would judge."

He better not, considering his bed is the one I do use on our trips. Not that Krista knows that.

And that isn't even the biggest secret I'm keeping from her. Not since I took that test.

For nine years, every time she and I have planned our trips to coincide with one of his concerts, I've had sex with her older brother. Mind-blowing, toe-curling, multiple-orgasming, scream-his-name sex.

"I know you two don't get along, but this is a big deal for him. Downfall's residency in Vegas means they don't have to tour so much. My mom is ecstatic that he's only a short plane ride away," she says.

Did I mention my partner in all that toe-curling sex is a guy I can't stand to have a conversation with? He's arrogant, entitled, and a downright jackass. Except in bed.

The first time it happened was absolutely a one-off. Too many shots of tequila. Too many snarky comments that caused his eyes to light up in a way that ignited a fire in my core and had my lady bits sitting up and begging like a puppy for a treat. It was only going to be the one time.

Then it happened again.

And then a third time. And, well, it kept happening. So much so that this year, I've been taking trips to meet up with him in other places on his tour. We've been scratching an itch that can't be soothed.

Or we *were*. Until those two fucking lines.

Now, though, I have a sneaking suspicion it's all over. I'm going to do the right thing and let him know. He can be involved or not. Either way, I'm keeping this baby. I've got a place to live back home in Aspen Falls, Colorado, and I've got a job working for my brother, Jagger.

I can do this.

On my own if I have to.

My stomach chooses that moment to gurgle and spin. I have thirty seconds to find a toilet or a trash can.

I bolt into the bathroom, making it in the nick of time to lose my meager lunch from the airport.

"Are you sick?" Krista follows me into the tiled room and lifts the hair off the back of my neck as I pray to the porcelain god in front of me.

"No," I gasp out between heaves. Once the universe grants me a reprieve from expunging my internal organs, I take several deep breaths. Then I grab several squares of toilet paper and wipe my mouth. "Probably motion sickness."

*You spelled morning sickness wrong.*

Only it isn't limited to the mornings. It's a whenever-it-feels-like-it level of hell that no one ever talks about.

"Do you need anything? Sprite? Ginger ale? Food?"

My stomach heaves at the mention of food, and I shake my head. "I think I just want my toothbrush and a nap before the show tonight."

"Yeah, sure. Wait right there." She bounces up like the Energizer Bunny.

I have no interest in waiting on the bathroom floor, so I stand and move toward the sink at a glacial pace.

Once I've got minty-fresh breath and feel more human, I wave her in the direction of the Strip visible outside our windows.

I can't say many nice things about Ryder. He's an asshole. Always has been. But he's not a cheap asshole. I'll give him credit for that.

"You should go have fun. Find your brother and catch up. It's been a while since you saw him."

The last time she and I attended a concert together was almost a year ago.

The last time *I* saw Ryder, though, was only eight weeks ago.

She studies me, worrying her lower lip. "Are you sure?"

"Positive." With a jaw-cracking yawn, I climb into bed and rest my head against the pillows.

"I should check in with him. Find out when Mom and Dad are arriving. He wants the whole family to see his first Vegas show. Isn't that sweet?"

More like he wants to show off for his family and his fans and be the perfect son.

"If you say so," I tell her, closing my eyes and sinking into the mattress.

"I wish the two of you could stand to be in the same room. I always wanted you to date. You'd have cute babies."

My eyes fly open, and I sit up. My heart practically leaps out of my chest as it takes off. "What?"

"You and Ryder," she says with a wicked smile. "You don't realize how good the two of you look together. I always thought—"

"Never gonna happen." The bitterness of the lie burns my throat.

She sighs. "I know, but a girl can wish, right? Okay, I'm gonna get out of here. Enjoy your nap."

She grabs her phone and purse, and between one breath and the next, she's out the door.

Hurricane Krista. The endearment fits her as much now as it did when Ryder coined it when we were nine.

What is he going to think of all this? I lift a hand to my still flat stomach and splay my fingers along the skin there.

"I guess we'll find out," I say out loud.

Drifting to sleep, I dream of our baby. Krista is right. Ryder and I do make beautiful babies.

What happens when Brittany spills her secret to Ryder? Grab ONE WEEKEND IN VEGAS available on Amazon and in KU and find out!

# PLAYLIST

The playlist for *Hating Mr. Write* is full of songs with personal meaning! Songs like "Fall Into Me" and "She's the One" by Brantley Gilbert were both ones sent to me by Dennis when we started dating. Then songs like "Hearts on Fire" by Illenium and "Labyrinth" by Taylor Swift give me the warm fuzzies.

Want to listen to the music inspired by Jagger and Hayley's love story? Check out the playlist on Spotify by searching for the "Hating Mr. Write" playlist or scan the QR code.

 You can both the playlist and the bonus tracks on my website:

https://www.breannalynnauthor.com

# ACKNOWLEDGMENTS

To you. Yes, you. The one who just read Jagger and Hayley and their happily ever after! Thank you for taking the chance on *Hating Mr. Write*. I hope you enjoyed reading this single mom story as much as I loved writing it!

To my family—thank you for being excited for me, for sharing my books, and for supporting me! I love you!

To Dennis—for being my real life book boyfriend and for loving my kids as much as you love me!

Claire and Alina—Special shout out to the two of you because you're you. Whether I'm writing or not, you love me! You also kick my butt when I should be writing. Love you both!

Isabelle—I meant what I said in the dedication. You wanted that perfect day. And it totally had me falling for Jagger even more than I had before.

For Ann R and Ann S—Thank you for being encouraging, for being patient, all your help, and comments on this manuscript! I'm so happy to work with you!

For Beth—your insights into my writing have continued to make me better. I couldn't do this without you!

Four years ago, I started this journey with serious thoughts of publishing. It has been a wild four years and I can't imagine doing any of it without you!

XOXO,
Breanna

# ALSO BY BREANNA LYNN

## HEART BEATS SERIES

*Written in the Beat*

*In The Beat of the Moment*

*Keeping the Beat*

*Betting on the Beat*

*Embracing the Beat*

*Falling for the Beat*

## SAFE HAVEN SECURITY

*Soldier for the Starling*

*Bodyguard for the Beauty Queen*

*Detective for the Debutante*

## STAND ALONE NOVELLAS

*Rockin' Around the Christmas Tree*

*Midnight in Mistletoe*

*Hating Mr. Write*

*One Weekend in Vegas*

# ABOUT THE AUTHOR

Breanna Lynn lives in Colorado with her two sets of twins (affectionately referred to as the Twinx), her boyfriend, his son, their two dogs, and three cats. A classy connoisseur of all things coffee, Breanna spends her free time keeping the Twinx from taking over the world. When not coordinating chaos, Breanna can be found binge reading, listening to music, or watching rom-coms with a giant bowl of popcorn.

Want to follow Breanna? Scan the QR code for all the ways to stay caught up!